"Let me go!"

"Wake up, Bethany. You're dreaming."

But still she fought, frantic with fear, her heart pounding a staccato rhythm against her ribs.

"It's only a dream," Tiger soothed her as he pulled her into his arms.

Bethany trembled against him, and he put one hand behind her head and drew her closer. Her body was warm against him, her tear-streaked face damp against his throat.

Suddenly an emotion he'd never known before swept through Tiger Malone. He whispered words that were a mixture of Chinese and English, trying to tell her that everything was all right, that he was with her now and that he would take care of her.

She leaned against him, and not even knowing that he was going to, he began to kiss the tears from her face. And finally, from her lips.

Dear Reader,

When two people fall in love, the world is suddenly new and exciting, and it's that same excitement we bring to you in Silhouette Intimate Moments. These are stories with scope, with grandeur. These characters lead the lives we all dream of, and everything they do reflects the wonder of being in love.

Longer and more sensuous than most romances, Silhouette Intimate Moments novels take you away from everyday life and let you share the magic of love. Adventure, glamour, drama, even suspense—these are the passwords that let you into a world where love has a power beyond the ordinary, where the best authors in the field today create stories of love and commitment that will stay with you always.

In coming months look for novels by your favorite authors: Maura Seger, Parris Afton Bonds, Elizabeth Lowell and Erin St. Claire, to name just a few. And whenever you buy books, look for all the Silhouette Intimate Moments, love stories *for* today's women *by* today's women.

Leslie J. Wainger
Senior Editor
Silhouette Books

IMRL-7/85

Barbara Faith
Kiss of the Dragon

Silhouette Intimate Moments

Published by Silhouette Books New York

America's Publisher of Contemporary Romance

Tyger! Tyger! burning bright
In the forests of the night,
What immortal hand or eye
Could frame thy fearful symmetry?

William Blake

To Neile J. (Mic) Kelsey,
number one cousin, brother, confidant, friend,
and a bit of a tiger himself

SILHOUETTE BOOKS
300 East 42nd St., New York, N.Y. 10017

Copyright © 1987 by Barbara Faith

ISBN: 0-373-07193-0

First Silhouette Books printing June 1987

BARBARA FAITH

is very happily married to an ex-matador whom she met when she lived in Mexico. After a honeymoon spent climbing pyramids in the Yucatán they settled down in California—but they're vagabonds at heart. They travel at every opportunity, but Barbara always finds the time to write.

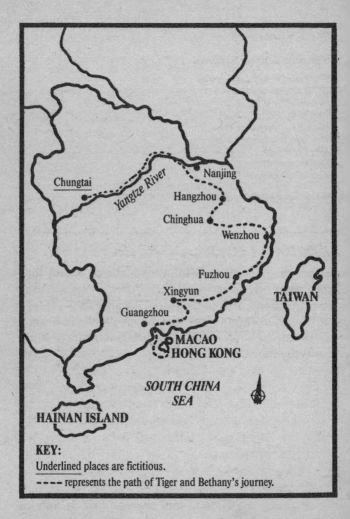

Chungtai

Yangtze River

Nanjing

Hangzhou

Chinghua

Wenzhou

Fuzhou

Xingyun

Guangzhou

MACAO
HONG KONG

TAIWAN

*SOUTH CHINA
SEA*

HAINAN ISLAND

KEY:

Underlined places are fictitious.

- - - - represents the path of Tiger and Bethany's journey.

Chapter 1

So this was Hong Kong, a bedazzlement of sights and sounds and aromas like no other place in the world. It wasn't anything like Tiffin, Ohio. The people that crowded the streets—a mixture of European, American, Chinese—were dressed in tailored suits, silk dresses, blue jeans, cheongsams and coolie outfits. Shops were blazoned with signs: Imperial Jade Company, Peter Choi Gems, Dim Sum Burger, Yue Po Chai Antiques, King Hueng Restaurant, Hong Kong Arts and Crafts. There was an aliveness here, an excitement that Bethany had never felt in any other city. For the first time she understood why her father had wanted her to come.

A lone rickshaw pulled away from the curb almost in front of them. The taxi driver yelled words Bethany didn't understand and swerved just in time to avoid a crash. The rickshaw driver, who couldn't have weighed more than a hundred and twenty pounds, shook his fist then stood arms akimbo in front of the taxi. Horns bleated behind them as her driver swerved around the rickshaw and headed back into the traffic.

She leaned forward in the cab, not wanting to miss anything, wondering what Hong Kong had been like when her father had been there almost forty years before.

For years she'd tried to get him to talk about his China days. But Ross Adams had been strangely reluctant to discuss them. He'd told her about Claire Chennault, of course, and he'd been proud to have been a member of the Flying Tigers in the days when China was at war with Japan. The United States had been China's ally then and Chennault had organized his Tigers to help Chiang Kai-shek's air force. Ross had liked flying in and out of China and he'd told Bethany that Hong Kong was the most exciting city in the world.

"There's nothing that can compare to the lights in Hong Kong harbor at night," he'd said. "No other feeling like being in Repulse Bay and looking out toward the South China Sea."

Then why, Bethany had asked him, had he left to go back to the States and settle in Tiffin, Ohio?

"I sure didn't plan to," Ross had told her with a sheepish smile. "I came back just to visit my folks after the war. But I met your mother and I stayed on. I talked to her about Hong Kong after we were married, but she didn't want any part of it. Said she'd been born and raised in Ohio and she wasn't going to leave it to go traipsing off to some godforsaken land where they ate chop suey three times a day."

Ross Adams had stayed in Tiffin and started a flying school. He liked his life well enough and everything had been fine up until a year ago. He'd started feeling the high cost of liability insurance, but had managed to keep his head above water until a larger, more modern flying school came to town. Business went downhill almost as rapidly as his health. Then Bethany's mother had surgery, followed by an incapacitating stroke. The combination just about finished him.

"I haven't done as well by you as I planned," he'd told Bethany a few weeks before he died. "I've got some money in the bank, but with your mother in the nursing home it won't last long." He reached for her hand. "But I've got something—something that's been hidden away for a long time, Bethy. It's worth a lot of money by now, maybe a couple of million dollars. After I'm gone I want you to go get it."

He'd told her then about Bill Malone. "Bill and I flew together," he said. "Flew in and out of China more times than I can count. Cracked up twice but we both managed to walk away from it. He met the prettiest Chinese girl I ever laid eyes on named Su Ching. Her father came from rich Manchurian people. After the war Bill and Su Ching got married and moved to Hong Kong."

Ross's eyes closed and he gripped hard on Bethany's hand. When he opened them he continued, "We did a lot of things I'm not especially proud of Bethy, black market stuff, same as everybody did in those days, booze, cigarettes, jade, silk." He sighed. "Made a lot of money, enough to set up business here and put some by. But not enough for what you're going to need to take care of your mother. That's why I want you to go to Hong Kong and find Bill Malone."

Bethany stared at him. "Go to Hong Kong? I can't leave you and mother."

"I'm not going to be around, honey, and your mother's being taken care of." He got up and belted the old flannel bathrobe around his frail body. He went to the rolltop desk in the alcove off the bedroom, opened a drawer on the right-hand side, felt around and pulled out a small wooden box. From it he took a gold key. Coming back to Bethany he placed it in her hand and closing her fingers around it said, "When I'm gone you get on the first plane out of here and head for Hong Kong. Find Bill. He'll have the other key. He'll take you to the dragon."

"The dragon?"

"The golden dragon, Bethy. It's been waiting all these years for someone to come and get it."

That day Hong Kong had seemed a million miles away. But here she was, trying to find a man by the name of Bill Malone.

The driver turned into Li Woo Street and slowed. "No houses," he said. "Only offices."

"Go further down." Bethany handed him the envelope her father had given her with Bill Malone's last address. "Number thirty-six."

"No thirty-six," he insisted. "All buildings."

"Please stop and ask."

The driver shrugged, then stopped. When he came back he gave the envelope back to Bethany and said,

"Houses torn down three years ago. No Bill Malone."

When Bethany got back to her hotel in Kowloon she looked in the phone book. There was one Malone listed. His name wasn't Bill and he didn't know anybody else by that name. She called the American Embassy and the man she talked to there said, "You might try the English-American Club. They'll have a list of members and perhaps your Mr. Malone is one of them."

"I've heard of a man named Malone," the woman Bethany spoke to at the English-American Club said. "But he's not one of our members." The way she said it made it sound as if she was glad he wasn't. "He owns a gambling club in Macao, The Golden Dragon." The woman sniffed audibly. "It's supposed to be the *in* place to go but you wouldn't catch me within a mile of it, or anywhere else in Macao for that matter."

Bethany thanked the woman and thoughtfully replaced the receiver. The Golden Dragon was a gambling club? Was that what her father had been talking about? But what did that have to do with a key? She sank down on her bed, knowing she had to go to Macao.

Quickly Bethany went downstairs to speak to the concierge. Macao was sixty kilometers from Hong Kong, he told her. Thirty-seven miles. Did madame wish to arrange for a tour?

Madame didn't. She wanted to go tonight and wondered if he would arrange for a taxi.

The concierge frowned. "I will arrange a taxi to take you to the pier, madame. From there you must take either a hydrofoil or a jet foil, which will take approximately forty minutes, or the ferry, which takes two and a half hours. But I would not advise you to go alone, especially at night." He hesitated. "Perhaps someone will meet you when you arrive?"

Now it was Bethany's turn to hesitate. She knew the concierge was only trying to be of assistance, but she had to find Bill Malone, and if going to Macao was the only way then she'd go to Macao. She thanked the concierge and told him that friends were meeting her.

At nine-thirty, wearing a turquoise silk pongee dress she'd bought yesterday in the hotel arcade, Bethany arrived at the pier and waited for the hydrofoil which was due to depart in fifteen minutes.

The Italian-built craft, appointed inside much like an airliner, set off across the water like a plane flying through turbulent air currents. A little under an hour later it arrived in Portuguese Macao. As the rest of the passengers disembarked, Bethany looked around and when the driver of a pedicab approached to ask, "Taxi, madame?" she nodded and said, "The Golden Dragon, please."

The streets of Macao were crowded, although it was past eleven, and for the first time since she'd left the hotel in Hong Kong, Bethany felt uncertain.

When the taxi pulled up in front of The Golden Dragon a doorman leaped forward to help her out. "Are you meeting someone here, madame?" he asked.

Bethany shook her head. "I've come to see Mr. Malone."

He held the door open and Bethany stepped into a strange world of red velvet and sparkling chandeliers.

She heard the excited murmur of voices, croupier calls, music, and the whir of roulette wheels. To her right there was a dimly lighted, crowded bar. Chinese cocktail waitresses in tight-fitting cheongsams flitted like colorful birds from table to table. In the foyer, on a marble pedestal, a five-foot golden dragon, its green eyes alight with an almost seductive gleam, stared at her.

Bethany took a step closer just as a voice said, "May I help you?"

The man, dressed in a dark-blue tuxedo, stood poised at the entrance to the main salon. "Are you looking for someone, madame?"

"No, I... yes." Bethany cleared her throat. "I'm looking for Mr. Malone. I was told that I could find him here."

"Do you have an appointment?"

"No, I'm afraid I don't. Is Mr. Malone here?"

"I will see, madame. May I have your name?"

"Bethany Adams. Please tell him I'm Ross Adams's daughter."

"Yes, madame. Will you wait in the bar while I see if Mr. Malone is available?"

"No, thank you. I'll just wait here if that's all right."

When he disappeared through a door across from the bar Bethany stepped closer to the dragon. He was as handsome as he was frightening. His green eyes glinted in the half light with a knowing, almost human look. She stared at him for a moment, feeling a strange fascination, then reluctantly turned away and moved closer to the entrance of the salon. The room was almost as large as the first floor of a department store. The chandeliers shone down on well-dressed men and women crowded around gaming tables. She caught snatches of conversation in English and Spanish and French, and other languages she didn't recognize. A cluster of small tables and chairs stood at the far end of the room, where couples were dancing to a five-piece band.

The door across from the bar opened. The maître d' beckoned and said, "Come with me, please."

Bethany gripped her white handbag as she stepped through the door into another foyer and followed the man up a broad circular staircase, then down a long corridor. He stopped at an ornately carved door at the end of the hall and knocked. He opened the door for Bethany to enter and closed the door behind her.

"You are Mr. Ross Adams's daughter?"

A man who had been seated behind a large rosewood desk at the other end of the room stood up and came toward her. He was tall and slender. His face had the classic cheekbones of a high-born Chinese and his green, almond-shaped eyes were slightly tilted. His black brocade dinner jacket and trousers were impeccably tailored and he was the most attractive man Bethany had ever seen, the epitome of everything she had ever imagined about the mysterious East.

She took the proffered hand and said, "Yes, I'm Bethany Adams. I'm sorry to bother you this way, but I'm looking for Mr. Malone."

"I'm Mr. Malone."

Bethany frowned and shook her head. "I'm looking for *Bill* Malone. He'd be about my father's age."

"Bill was my father. He died almost three years ago." He took her arm and led her to a black velvet sofa. "My name is Tiger, Miss Adams—and if you even chuckle I won't give you a drop of the champagne I opened when I heard you were here." He smiled as he took a bottle from an ice bucket, filled two golden goblets, and handed one to her. "Is this your first visit to Hong Kong?" he asked.

"Yes." Bethany looked at him over the rim of her goblet. He spoke with an English accent, but his appearance hinted at another, older culture. "I'm staying in Kowloon. I took a hydrofoil to come here tonight."

"You came alone?"

Bethany's hands tightened around the goblet. "Yes."

He looked slightly puzzled. "Is your father in Hong Kong with you?"

"No, Mr. Malone, he died a month ago."

"I'm sorry. I've heard a lot about him. My father loved to talk about their days together. It's too bad the two of them never got together after the war."

Bethany nodded as she sipped the champagne, wondering what she should do next. Should she give Bill Malone's son her father's letter and the key or just thank him for the drink and leave? Her hands closed around her purse. She didn't know what was in the letter, only that a lot of money was involved and that she had to go cautiously.

The telephone rang. While Tiger answered it Bethany took a moment to look around her. The office was large and plushly decorated, its paneled walls lined with books and jade figurines. When he replaced the phone he added more champagne to Bethany's goblet. "You didn't come to Hong Kong expressly to see my father, did you?"

"No," Bethany said, a shade too quickly. She stood up. "I don't want to bother you, Mr. Malone. I know you're busy."

"Not that busy. Please, finish your champagne and I'll show you around the club."

Tiger observed Bethany as she sipped her drink and found her an unusually lovely woman. Small boned, with delicate features, her eyes were wide and gray, her hair the color of sun-ripened wheat, and she had the best-looking pair of legs he'd ever seen. He didn't think she could be more than twenty-three or -four. There was an air of freshness about her that pleased him. He wondered what had brought her to Hong Kong alone.

When Bethany finished her champagne Tiger took her arm and said, "Come along. Let me give you a tour."

"I really should be getting back to my hotel."

"I will take you back whenever you're ready." He smiled at her. "Our fathers were friends, Miss Adams; they'd want me to look after you. And I can't keep calling you Miss Adams. What is your first name?"

"Bethany."

Tiger nodded with approval. "That suits you." He led her downstairs to a table near the band. He signaled to a waiter and ordered a bottle of wine and a light supper. "I will be back soon," he said.

When he had attended to his business he returned. "Have you ever been in a gambling club before?" he asked while the waiter served them.

"We don't have too many gambling clubs in Tiffin," Bethany said with a smile. "Is all this yours?"

"Every roulette wheel and slot machine. My father wanted me to be a flyer so he taught me to fly when I was fifteen. I like flying but I think I would have liked it more in the days when he and your dad were flying with the Tigers." He sighed. "That's how I got the name. I was a souvenir from his days with Chennault." He looked at her curiously. "Did your father tell you much about all that?"

"Not until just a short time before he died. He spoke a lot about your father then. He told me that your mother was Chinese and that she was one of the most beautiful women he'd ever seen."

"She is French-Chinese, and yes, she's very beautiful. She lives in Guantung Province over in mainland China. Do you plan to visit China during your stay in Hong Kong?"

"I...I don't think so."

"I would like to show you around while you're here. Are you free for lunch tomorrow?" Before she could answer he said, "I'll pick you up at twelve." He stood up. "Shall we dance?"

Tiger was tall. His body was lean and when he put his arms around Bethany she could feel the ripple of muscle under the tailored jacket. For some inexplicable reason she suddenly felt like a freshman at a senior prom, awkward and unsure of herself, totally out of her element. It was this place, all the glitter and glamour, she told herself. It was too exotic, too... Bethany looked up at Tiger and felt the breath catch in her throat. He was so unlike any man she'd ever known before. The slight tilt only made his eyes more mysteriously attractive. He had an aristocratic nose, and his mouth . . . She took a deep breath and moved farther away from him.

If Tiger noticed the movement he didn't mention it. They finished their dance and after they'd had their coffee he asked someone to get a taxi.

They arrived at the dock just in time to catch the jet foil. When they disembarked they took a taxi to the Star Ferry. There Tiger took Bethany's arm and led her down a passage to the turnstiles.

"Would you prefer to be upstairs in first class?" he asked. "Or would you like to be close to the water?"

"Close to the water sounds lovely." Bethany moved to the rail and breathed in the sharp salt air.

The spring night was soft with the promise of summer. Lights sparkled down from the surrounding hills, reflecting, dancing on the water. Other lights beckoned from the distant shore. It was long past midnight but motorboats, ferries, sampans and square-bowed junks plied their way back and forth in the harbor. With a sigh Bethany leaned against the railing, letting the breeze blow the hair back from her face.

"I can smell the sea," she said as she leaned forward. Suddenly, tears welled in her eyes.

Tiger put his hand on her shoulder. "What is it?" he asked in a gentle voice.

"My father," Bethany said with a shaking sigh. "He wanted me to see this, that's why he insisted I come. And now . . . now I'm so glad I did because it's almost as though he were here with me."

Tiger put a finger under her chin and raised her face so that he could look at her. "Is that the only reason you came to Hong Kong, Bethany?" he asked.

She looked into his eyes and for a moment she was tempted to tell him the real reason. But only for a moment. Then she stepped away from him and wiping her eyes said, "Yes, that's the only reason."

Tiger didn't believe her, but he let it go. He put his arm around her and they stood by the railing as the lights of Kowloon grew close.

When they went in to her hotel Tiger meant only to walk her to the elevators, but as they started across the lobby he noticed a Chinese man sitting to one side reading a newspaper. As they passed him he lowered the paper and casually stood up. Tiger's hand tightened on Bethany's arm. He'd seen the man before. A week ago the same man had visited the casino. His bets had been small and Tiger wouldn't have remembered him at all if one of the croupiers hadn't told him that the man had made inquiries about his father.

"He wanted to know if he was the Malone who flew with the Tigers," the croupier said. "I told him I didn't know."

Now the same man was here, waiting in the lobby of Bethany's hotel, and Tiger didn't like it.

When they reached the elevators he said to Bethany, "I'll see you to your door."

"That's not necessary." She tried to step away from him but he kept hold of her arm. The doors opened and they stepped inside. The Chinese man who'd been watching them looked the other way.

At Bethany's door Tiger said, "Be sure to lock your door when you go in."

"Yes, of course." She looked at him curiously. "Is there any particular reason why I should?"

Tiger smiled. "Don't you know that Hong Kong is filled with opium-smoking white slavers?"

Bethany smiled back. "Really? How fascinating. I had an Aunt Christine who used to warn me about white slavers every time I wanted to go to a Saturday matinee."

Tiger's lips twitched. "She did well to warn you." He took her hand. "I will see you tomorrow. Is twelve o'clock agreeable?"

"Twelve o'clock is fine." Bethany looked at him, then away. When she was safely in her room she leaned her back against the door, not sure whether she was relieved or happy that Tiger hadn't tried to kiss her.

The Chinese man was still in the lobby when Tiger got off the elevator. He had a drink beside him now and seemed engrossed in his newspaper. But as Tiger went out the revolving door the man quickly folded his newspaper and rose to follow him.

Chapter 2

Bethany's first conscious thought when she awoke the next morning was of Tiger Malone. With a sleepy sigh she closed her eyes and conjured up his face; hair as black as a crow's wing, high cheekbones and the slight, exotic tilt to the green eyes that made him look so sensually mysterious. He was a little over six feet tall, his body was lean and muscular. Bethany knew almost nothing about him except that he was Bill Malone's son and that he owned a gambling club. But he was the most exciting man she'd ever known and in a little more than three hours she was going to see him again.

Tiger was waiting in the lobby when Bethany came out of the elevator at five minutes to twelve. His glance swept her pink pleated skirt and matching short-sleeved sweater approvingly before he handed her a small package and said, ''I took the liberty of buying you a scarf. It will probably be windy where we're going."

"Thank you." She looked at him quickly, then fumbled with the red string as she unwrapped the tissue paper and saw the blue silk scarf.

"It's lovely, Mr. Malone . . . Tiger. Thank you."

"You're welcome." He took her arm. "We are going to have lunch up at Victoria Peak. You can get a three-hundred-and-sixty-degree view of just about the whole territory from there. If it's clear we will be able to see some of the South China Sea Islands."

South China Sea Islands. A shiver of excitement ran up Bethany's spine. Hong Kong, Macao, the South China Sea Islands! She took a deep breath, still not quite able to believe she was actually here, feeling more alive than she'd ever felt before as Tiger led her out of the hotel to the pleasantly noisy street.

They spoke little as they walked with the flow of traffic. The streets were thronged with people, many of them tourists, gawking along with Bethany at the shop windows and street displays. When finally they reached the foot of Victoria Peak they took a tram on a shaky, almost vertical ride to the top.

"Better put your scarf on," Tiger said as they stepped out of the tram. "It's usually windy up here."

It was windy—but breathtaking. The view stretched as far as Bethany could see; Hong Kong Harbor and the city lay spread out below, beyond lay the mountains and behind the mountains mainland China.

"This is called Victoria Peak because Hong Kong was acquired by the British during that queen's reign," Tiger told Bethany. "But soon they will leave and China will take over."

"How do you feel about that?" Bethany asked curiously.

"I have mixed feelings." Tiger hesitated. "It's going to be difficult for many of the Hong Kong people. Even though they have been under British rule, they're not wanted in Britain. A lot of the people here fled from mainland China and they fear what will happen to them when China takes over in 1997."

"What about you? Your father was an American. Do you have an American passport?"

Tiger nodded. "But I am not sure that makes me an American. I was born in China. I spoke Chinese before I spoke English. When I finally began to speak English it was with a British-Chinese accent. I went to prep school in England then on to Cambridge." He brushed his wind-ruffled hair back off his forehead. "But that does not make me British either, does it? So if I'm not American or British, what am I? Chinese?" He shook his head. "I get along in China and I love my mother very much, but I don't belong there and I wouldn't want to live there."

"Have you ever been to the United States?"

"Once for a year when I was ten. My father wanted me to go to school in Boston. He was raised there and he had some good memories of the city." Tiger gripped the rail in front of them. "But I don't have good memories. I was the strange boy in school because I didn't look like everybody else. I hated it. I'll never go back."

Only a few moments before Bethany had thought of Tiger Malone as a supremely sophisticated man of the world. Now she saw the hidden hurt and the vulnerability. She wanted to reach out and touch him, to comfort the strange boy who looked just different enough from the other boys to have become the brunt of jibes and jokes. Instead she said, "It's always hard to be either new or different, Tiger. Children can be terrible sometimes." With a quick smile she added, "I have a feeling that things might have changed now. You really ought to give us another chance."

"Perhaps I will some day." Then, ending the conversation, he took her arm and led her into the restaurant. He spoke of other things and while Bethany listened she tried to understand this impeccably dressed man who had been strong enough to share his vulnerability with her. There was something about him, an air of dignity and of an old-world courtliness that was a rare commodity in the twentieth-century male.

When they finished lunch Tiger said, "I thought we might drive out to Repulse Bay." At Bethany's confused look he added, "It's named for a British man-o'-war. The area is a residential district now. I'd like to show you where I live."

Tiger noticed the alarm in her gray eyes, as she hesitated, then looked at her watch and said, "I really should be getting back to the hotel."

For a moment he ached to put his arms around her. There was an aura of innocence about her that excited him, and he wondered what it would be like to hold her, to kiss those sweetly curved, slightly parted lips.

He took her hand when they left the restaurant and held it all the way down in the tram.

* * *

When they drove around the curve of Repulse Bay Tiger pulled into a turnoff. When he helped Bethany out of the car he recaptured her hand and held it as she gazed out over the harbor.

"That's the entrance to the South China Sea," he said.

"It must be the most beautiful view in the world." Bethany took a deep breath as she looked down at the harbor where pleasure boats and sampans bobbed gently on the blue-green water. A little beyond them a yacht was moored, sparkling white against the water, beautifully rich and opulent.

"Wouldn't you like to see where I live?" Tiger asked. Not waiting for an answer he led her back to the car, but instead of driving up to the houses he drove down to the harbor. When he parked and opened her door, Bethany looked at him inquiringly and said, "I thought we were going to your home."

"We are." He motioned to one of the sampans and spoke in Chinese to the old woman who sat cross-legged on the bow. The woman quickly pulled the sampan up to the dock. Tiger took Bethany's hand and helped her into the boat.

"Where are we going?" she asked.

"To my home." Tiger smiled and pointed to the yacht she'd seen from above.

Bethany stared at him as the sampan maneuvered around the other boats in the harbor, then turned to gaze at the beautiful craft. There was a slight chop to the deep blue water, and overhead white puffs of clouds drifted slowly along.

The sampan approached from the bow and when they were in shouting distance Tiger called out, "Ahoy the *Dragon*!" A Chinese man appeared, saluted, then quickly lowered a boarding ramp. She took the man's proffered hand as Tiger said, "This is Miss Bethany Adams, Chang. Bethany, this is Chang Lu, my number one man."

"How do you do?" Bethany said as the man bowed.

"Welcome to the *Golden Dragon*, Miss Adams," Chang Lu said with a British accent. "Let me help you aboard." Then to Tiger he said, "Why didn't you let me know you were coming? Lee would have prepared lunch."

"We've already had lunch, but if I can persuade Miss Adams to stay we would like a light supper later."

Chang bowed. "I will tell Lee." He motioned to Bethany. "Please, come this way. It is cooler inside."

Bethany walked across the teak deck and stepped through sliding glass doors onto a thick red carpet. A large, L-shaped white sofa decorated with gold pillows and flanked by two white chairs dominated the room. A bowl of scarlet poppies rested on a lacquer coffee table, and there were matching gold lily lamps on either side of the sofa. Chinese paintings decorated the walls; beneath one there was an ornately carved Chinese trunk, beneath the other a desk. At the far end of the room there was a stairway.

"The stairway leads to a lounge," Tiger said. "It's a pleasant place to watch television and have a drink when the weather is bad. The dining room is up there too, but if it's warm tonight we will eat outside on the aft deck. The sunsets in this part of the world are spectacular.''

Everything's spectacular, Bethany thought.

"May I fix you a drink?" Chang asked.

"No, thank you."

"Then why don't we have coffee?" Tiger took Bethany's hand and led her to the sofa. "What do you think of my home?" he asked with a smile.

"It's beautiful! How long have you lived here?"

"For almost three years. I bought it at a very good price from one of my customers who was having a streak of bad luck. I didn't plan to live on it. Then when I did I thought it would be only for a month or two, until I sold it. Chang and Lee were on the boat when I bought it and I asked them to stay on." He smiled at Bethany. "They spoiled me. I found that this was a haven, far enough away from the club to give me a feeling of escape. I keep an apartment in Macao, but this as my home."

"Do you take trips . . . cruises, I mean?"

"Once in a while. The *Dragon*'s a sixty-three-foot Hatteras, built to go anywhere, but so far I've only taken short cruises. Sometime I'd like to take a longer trip."

Chang brought a silver tray and placed it on the coffee table in front of them. "I brought the Spanish brandy and some fruit that I thought Miss Adams might enjoy."

"Thank you, Chang," Tiger said as the Chinese man bowed and left the salon. When they were alone he poured Bethany's coffee and turning to her said, "Now, why don't you tell me the real reason you came to Hong Kong?"

Bethany's eyes widened. Tiger **had taken** her off guard and for a moment she was too surprised to answer. She studied Tiger over the rim of her coffee cup. She didn't know him very well, but there was something about him that inspired trust. Her father had told her to give the letter and the key to Bill Malone. Bill Malone was dead, but his son was alive.

"My father wrote a letter to your father," she said at last. "That's why I came to Hong Kong. He wanted me to give the letter to him." She hesitated, then she opened her purse, took out the letter and handed it to Tiger.

He held it for a moment, then slit the letter open with his thumbnail. When he saw the gold key his hand tightened around it and he shot a quick look at Bethany. "Would you like to read the letter, or shall I?"

"You read it, please." Bethany's hands were shaking.

Tiger nodded and began to read aloud:

"Dear Bill,

"It's been a long time. I've been meaning to write for a year but I kept waiting for things to get better. But things aren't getting better so before my time runs out I'd better tell you how it is.

"I told you the last time I wrote that my flying school was doing real well. But a year ago a big outfit from Chicago came to town and damn near ruined me. I might have been able to hold out if it hadn't been for liability insurance. That broke my back, Bill, and I had to throw the towel in. Then six months ago Mary Elizabeth had surgery and just as she started feeling better she had a stroke. She's in a nursing home now and the doctors say it's only a matter of time for her.''

Tiger glanced up at Bethany. ''That's your mother?''

She nodded, unable to speak as she clasped her hands together.

Tiger covered her hands with one of his, then continued.

''When things start going downhill they seem to pick up speed, old buddy. I started feeling like hell right about the time I found out about Mary Elizabeth. A couple of weeks ago the doc told me I had about three months left. That's why I'm writing this letter. I'm giving it to my daughter and I want her to take it to you.

''Bethy's a real good girl, Bill. But her mother and I have overprotected her and I just don't know how she's going to do on her own. One thing for damn sure, she's going to be stone-cold broke. That's why I'm sending her to you, partner. It's time to go after the dragon.

''I know we said we wouldn't go after it unless we were desperate. Well I guess I'm just about as desperate as a man can get. I'm dying and Bethy's mother needs more money for her care than I can manage. I want my little girl taken care of. I know going after the dragon will be risky, but if you can get it and get out all in one piece you and Su Ching and your son and Bethy will be set for life. You take care of my girl, Bill, she's all that's

left of me and Mary Elizabeth. She's the best of
both of us.''

Tiger laid the letter on the lacquer table. He looked
at Bethany, saw the glint of tears in her eyes, and
poured a splash of brandy into one of the glasses and
handed it to her.

When she had taken a sip she asked, "Do you know
anything about the dragon?"

Tiger nodded. "I heard my father speak of it to my
mother. But whenever he did her face would stiffen
and she'd become angry. When I was older he told me
stories about it. I guess that's why I named the club
and this boat the *Golden Dragon*."

He got up suddenly and went to stand before one of
the windows. He looked out and for a long moment he
didn't speak.

It was quiet in the salon. Bethany could feel the
slight motion of the waves and hear the splash of water against the hull when a boat headed out of the
harbor. She swirled the brandy in her snifter, waiting
for Tiger to speak.

Finally he turned to her and said, "I asked you once
if your father ever spoke of the time he spent in China
with the Flying Tigers. Do you know anything at all
about those days, Bethany?"

She shook her head. "I know Dad was one of the
Flying Tigers, but that's about all because he never
seemed to want to talk about it. I've read about the
Tigers, enough to know that General Chennault
formed the group to help Chiang Kai-shek against the
Japanese. Dad mentioned once that at first he flew out
of a place called Hengchow and that later the head-

quarters were in Kunming. I've seen pictures of the planes—with the shark mouths painted on them but I never understood why they used a shark if they were called Flying Tigers.''

"The tiger is the national symbol of China," he explained, "and the shark was considered bad luck to the maritime Japanese.'' He came back to the sofa and stood looking down at her for a moment. "Those were dangerous years, Bethany," he said at last. "Half of the planes the men flew looked as though they belonged in a museum. Most of the time they couldn't get spare parts; they went into the air on the proverbial wing and a prayer. The runways were almost as dangerous as the Japanese. It took sixty days for 120,000 coolies to scratch out a runway in Hengchow.'' Tiger's black brows came together in a frown as he shook his head. "Can you imagine what it must have been like? How dangerous it was trying to fight an aerial war in those beat-up, patched-up planes? Landing on bumpy, rock-strewn airstrips in the middle of nowhere?''

Tiger poured a small amount of brandy for himself and drank it down. "But the Tigers hung on, even when Shanghai fell in 1937 and Chungking became the Nationalist war capital. What they lacked in military discipline they made up for in courage.'' He took her hand. "Our fathers were brave men; they did a lot of things we should be proud of.''

Her eyes were moist. "I know," she said in a shaky voice.

"But they did other things, things that were not always honorable, that in those days were an accepted way of life.''

"I don't understand. What are you trying to tell me?"

"That both of our fathers engaged in smuggling."

"Smuggling?" Bethany glared at him. "They may have traded on the black market but that wasn't really smuggling."

"Wasn't it? Whatever you choose to call it, Bethany, it was illegal. They smuggled jewels, works of art, gold and fine silks. They made a lot of money, enough for both of our fathers to go into business after the war."

Bethany's gray eyes narrowed in anger. "Are you trying to tell me my father was a crook?" she snapped.

"No, I'm trying to tell you the way it was." Tiger stood up abruptly and said, "Let's get some air." He took her hand and led her out of the salon onto the deck. As they stood looking out over the water Tiger continued, "Your father sent you to Hong Kong because there was something he wanted you to know, something he wanted you to do."

When Bethany didn't answer Tiger put his hands on her shoulders and turned her so that she would face him. "We cannot judge what our fathers did because the times were so different then. They lived with danger every day of their lives. Perhaps the excitement of smuggling... of black marketeering took their minds off the fact that the next time they went up they might never come back."

Bethany tried to step away from him, but Tiger held her. "One of the things they smuggled was a statue from the Sung dynasty. Warlords had been fighting over it since the eleventh century. It has fallen into many different hands in the last few hundred years and caused many deaths.''

Bethany tried to struggle out of his grip but his hands tightened. "The statue is of a golden dragon. Our fathers brought it from Sichuan to Nanchang on consignment. But the man who hired them was murdered before they could deliver it. So they kept it.'' His voice lowered to an almost whisper. "Forty years ago the golden dragon had a market value of half a million dollars. Today its value has quadrupled.''

Tiger released his grip on her arms. "The golden dragon is in China, Bethany, in the same place our fathers hid it over forty years ago.''

"But if...'' Bethany moistened her lips. "But if what you say is true, why didn't they take it out years ago?''

"There was a war going on. They couldn't have sold anything that valuable at that time, so they left it there until after the war. But after the war the world changed; China became a communist country and Chiang Kai-shek fled to Taiwan. China was closed to foreigners, and no one could get in or out.''

"But China opened up later,'' Bethany said. "Why didn't they go after it then?''

"I have asked myself the same question. The only reason I could come up with is that maybe, after all these years, they realized how dangerous it might be to go after it.''

"Dangerous?'' Bethany looked at him. "But my father gave me the key. He wanted me to get the statue.''

"It will take two keys to open the place where it is hidden," Tiger said. "I have the other key. I will go after the dragon."

Bethany took a deep breath to steady herself because she knew that what he'd told her was true. She believed there really was a golden dragon. And if there was, then part of it belonged to her, as part of the risk belonged to her.

She looked into his jade-green eyes and said, "When you go after the dragon, I'm going with you."

Chapter 3

That's impossible!"

"Why?" Bethany faced him, hands on her hips, chin thrust forward.

"Because it will probably be dangerous."

She shook her head impatiently, obvious disbelief written on her face. "If you're willing to face danger to claim your half of the dragon then so am I. If the dragon is where our fathers left it we just go and get it. We..." She stopped. "You *do* know where the dragon is, don't you?"

Tiger shook his head. "But I'm sure my mother does. I think she has known for years but she has never touched it because she disapproved when our fathers decided to keep the dragon." He faced Bethany. "I will go to Kwantung and talk to Mother and tell her about you. I will show her your father's letter and she will understand that it is time to get the dragon." Tiger hesitated, then attempting to make Bethany understand said, "If there is any danger it's better that I go alone, no one will be curious about me. I'm half Chinese and can move about freely. I'll get the dragon and bring it back here to Hong Kong. Then we'll locate a dealer, and when it's sold we'll divide whatever it brings."

Bethany nodded. "That part's agreeable, Tiger. But not the part about your going to China alone. When you go I'm going with you."

Tiger's jaw clenched. "No, you're not," he said firmly. "You will stay here in Hong Kong and wait until I return."

"No, I won't!"

Tiger glared at her. Her father had said she'd been overprotected and that he didn't know how she'd manage on her own, but from the fiery look in her eyes Tiger had a hunch she'd manage very well.

They argued for most of the afternoon. Tiger tried first to be quietly reasonable; when this tactic failed, he alternated between pleading and anger. He rarely allowed himself to be angry but Bethany infuriated him. No matter what he said she remained calm, but adamant. She *was* going to China with him. She *was* going to help him find the dragon. Nothing he could say would dissuade her.

So Tiger decided to stop arguing. The solution was simple; he would agree to take her. Then he would leave the day before they were scheduled to depart, and by the time Bethany discovered she'd been tricked he'd be halfway to China.

They sat on the aft deck that night. Tiger introduced her to his cook, Lee Tung, a small, rotund man who smiled and bowed and said that he had prepared a most simple dinner. This proved to be cold lobster with hollandaise sauce, hearts of palm salad, French bread and chilled white wine. For dessert there was a white chocolate mousse and coffee.

When the dishes had been taken away Bethany leaned back in her chair. Lights blinked from the distant shore. A yellow slice of new moon, lone companion to the myriad stars, seemed painted on the evening sky. She'd never known anything could be this peaceful, this beautiful. The slight motion of the boat had a calming, lulling effect.

With a sigh she said, "I'd better go before I fall asleep."

"You're welcome to stay. I have three staterooms. I will drive you back to Kowloon tomorrow when I go to Macao."

"No thank you." The idea of spending a night here on the boat with Tiger Malone both frightened and excited her. Then she remembered that if she sailed to China she'd be spending a lot of nights with him. But not tonight.

They had little to say on the way back to her hotel. Again, as he had done the night she'd come to the club, Tiger parked on the Hong Kong side so that they could take the ferry to Kowloon.

It wasn't until they were on the ferry that Tiger became aware of the two men watching them. At first he paid no attention. Bethany was an unusually pretty young woman, so it was only natural that men would look at her. He liked looking at her himself.

But Tiger took her arm when they left the boat, deliberately slowing his steps and pausing to point out the lights on the other side of the harbor.

The two men also paused.

Tiger's hand tightened on Bethany's arm. He didn't want to alarm her but the hour was late and he felt a sudden need to get away from this darkened dock area.

When he quickened his pace she looked up at him. "What is it?" she said curiously.

"Nothing, it's late. We'd better—"

A rough hand on Tiger's shoulder whirled him around. Bethany gasped, then screamed as the second man tried to grab her purse. She hit him with the back of her hand and tried to pull away, quickly taking in the man's appearance. She struck him again and he grabbed a handful of her hair. She kicked, connecting with his shin. Out of the corner of her eye she saw Tiger and another man fighting, heard the sound of fist against jaw. The other man grunted, staggered back a few steps, fell to his knees, then flat on his face.

Tiger spun around, grabbed the man Bethany had been struggling with, hit him in the throat with the edge of his hand and followed it up with a chop behind the man's ear. Her assailant fell without a sound.

Bethany stared down at the two men, and took a deep breath to steady herself. "They...they wanted my purse," she said.

"Are you all right? Did he hurt you?"

"No, I don't think so."

"Then let's get the hell out of here."

Tiger hurried her along the dock to the Hong Kong Hotel, entered, cut through the coffee shop to the lobby, then out to the well-lighted street. He tried to tell himself that the two men who jumped them were purse-snatchers, but he couldn't quite convince himself. Purse-snatchers usually hit and ran. Unless they were desperate they rarely wanted to fight. But these men had been serious; they wanted Bethany's purse and they were willing to fight for it. Tiger's steps quickened.

When they reached Bethany's hotel he said, "I'm coming up with you."

Bethany looked at him, surprised. "There's no need, I'm a little shaky but I'll be all right." A little shaky! Now that it was over she wasn't sure her legs would hold her as far as the elevator.

Tiger tightened his hand on her arm, and with a smile he said, "You surprised me. You appear to be very fragile but you put up a pretty good fight."

"I surprised myself. I know you're not supposed to resist, but everything I've got—airline tickets, traveler's checks, money, passport, Dad's letter, is in my purse. I was darned if I was going to give it up without a fight."

They reached her door and she took the key out and handed it to Tiger. He opened the door, stepped inside and felt on the wall for the light switch.

"Thank you for seeing me home. I'll..." She gasped and grabbed his arm. "My God!" she whispered. "Look at the room."

Her clothes lay in a jumbled heap on the floor. The dresser drawers had been pulled out, and the contents carelessly spilled. The mirror over the dresser had been ripped from the wall and the back of it slashed. The

lamp on the nightstand beside her bed was overturned, the bed covers thrown back.

"Stay right here," Tiger murmured. He checked the
corridor, closed the door, then silently crossed the
room. He inspected the bathroom, then moved to the
balcony, slid back the glass doors and stepped out.

Bethany stood frozen, hands clenched tightly to her
sides. She'd never seen anything like this before. The
room was a mess, her clothes scattered. She had no
idea what might be missing. Had the burglars been
looking for money? For jewelry? Why had they picked
her room to rob?

Tiger came back into her room and beckoned her
inside. "Pack your things," he said. "You're coming
back to the boat with me."

Bethany looked at him in shock, unable to speak for
a moment, her gray eyes wide as she stared up into
Tiger's face. "Shouldn't we call the police?" she asked
in a shaking voice.

"We will leave that to the hotel." Tiger strode to the
closet. Her suitcase and overnight bag were on the
floor. The lining had been ripped out but they were
usable. He looked at Bethany. She was pale and he
knew she was close to breaking down. He put the
suitcases on the bed and trying to jar her snapped,
"Don't just stand there, help me pack."

Bethany sank down on the bed beside her clothes.
"Maybe if I move to another room—?"

"No, not another room. You're coming with me."
He didn't want to frighten her but he didn't like what
had happened—first the two men jumping them on
the dock, now this. He wanted Bethany where he knew
she'd be safe; he wanted her on his boat.

Bethany argued even as she helped him throw her things into her suitcase. Then, before Tiger could stop her she went into the bathroom to get her toilet articles. With a cry she slumped against the door. The bathroom looked worse than the other room. Her jar of cold cream had been broken and the cream smeared on the rug. Everything had been broken and emptied.

Bethany fell to her knees with a cry and began trying to clean the rug with a towel, not even aware that tears were running down her face. When Tiger lifted her to her feet she said, "No, let me go, I have to clean it up."

Tiger said, "Don't worry Bethany. Leave it." He led her out of the bathroom and helped her gather the things that were still usable. When they were packed he called Macao and spoke to the manager of The Golden Dragon and told him that he wouldn't be in tonight. Then he called down to the desk, telling them that Miss Adams's room had been ransacked, that she was leaving, and that they would be down in a moment to check out.

When they stopped at the desk the manager apologized and offered another room. Tiger declined and led Bethany out of the hotel to a taxi.

She was silent on the way back to his boat, exhausted by what had happened, willing for the moment to let him take care of her. She'd stay on the boat, for tonight at least and tomorrow she'd find another hotel.

Once again a sampan took them out to Tiger's boat, and once again Chang Lu greeted them. If he was surprised to see Bethany he didn't show it. He took her bags when Tiger said, "Put them in the stateroom next to mine, Chang." Then Tiger led Bethany to the sofa, poured two brandies, and handed her one.

She'd held up remarkably well after what had happened. She hadn't fallen apart after the attack on the dock or when she'd walked into her hotel room and found everything turned upside down. But the strain showed in her pallor.

He was glad she was here with him and he would keep her here for as long as necessary to be sure she was safe. The two attacks worried him more than he liked to admit. The one on the dock might have been because Bethany looked like a typical American tourist, but the ransacking of her room was too much of a coincidence. No, he couldn't believe it was because she was a tourist. They—whoever they were—had been after something.

Tiger's face tightened. For the past few weeks he had suspected that he was being followed, but he'd told himself it was because of the club. There were always a few disgruntled patrons, perhaps one of them had decided either to steal the lost money back or take revenge on the owner of The Golden Dragon.

But he didn't think what had happened tonight had anything to do with the club.

"I don't want to impose," Bethany said, breaking in on his thoughts. "I'll stay tonight if you insist but tomorrow I'll find another hotel."

"We will talk about it in the morning. Now why don't you try to get some sleep?"

"Yes, I think I will." Bethany took another sip of her brandy and set the glass on the coffee table. Tiger led her through the salon and down a short flight of stairs to the staterooms.

"If you want anything I will be right next door," Tiger said. He put his hand on her shoulder. "Try to rest, Bethany. Don't think about what has happened. You're safe here."

She heard the growl of motors and the boat began to move. "What's happening?" she asked nervously. "Why are we moving?"

"I've asked Chang to take us farther out in the bay. It will be quieter." Tiger didn't add that he'd also told Chang to stand watch. He opened the cabin door. "Try to rest," he said, "you'll feel better in the morning."

The stateroom was almost the size of her bedroom back home. The double bed was built flush against the wall. There was a built-in dressing table and a chair that was fastened to the floor. Her clothes had been hung in the closet and what was left of her toilet articles placed in the adjoining bathroom. In spite of her weariness Bethany smiled. If this was how the other half lived she just might learn to like it.

After Bethany had bathed and slipped into her nightgown she turned out the overhead light and opened the curtains that covered the porthole. A soft breeze cooled the cabin, the gentle movement of the water soothed her. Trying not to think of the attack on the dock or of the ruined hotel room, she closed her eyes. But it was a long time before she was able to sleep.

She dreamed of shop windows filled with exotic things—beautiful gowns, cool jade and sparkling jewels. A shopkeeper appeared. He pointed to the most beautiful dress Bethany had ever seen and crooking a finger motioned her inside his shop. But once inside the beautiful dress and the shopkeeper disappeared. She was on the dock and it was night. Lights shone dimly through a fog and suddenly she heard footsteps. She tried to run but couldn't; her feet were so heavy that she could barely lift them. The footsteps grew closer. She moaned in fear and tried with every ounce of strength to move her leaden feet. Slowly, oh so slowly, she began to run. The footsteps grew closer. Closer. A hand reached for her, held her. "Let me go! Let me go!" she screamed and fought to break free, crying, "Please let me go!"

"Bethany!"

"Let me go!"

"Wake up, Bethany. You're dreaming."

But still she fought, frantic with fear, her heart pounding a staccato rhythm against her ribs.

"It's only a dream," Tiger soothed her as he pulled her into his arms.

Bethany trembled against him and he put one hand behind her head and drew her closer. Her body was warm against him, her tear-streaked face damp against his throat. Suddenly an emotion he'd never known before swept through Tiger Malone. He whispered words that were a mixture of Chinese and English, trying to tell her that everything was all right, that he was with her now and that he would take care of her.

She sighed against him, and not even knowing that he was going to, he began to kiss the tears from her face. And finally from her lips.

Lips that quivered under his as her body tensed and she tried to move away. Tiger's arms tightened around her. He looked down into her face. Her eyes, shadowed by the moonlight, were wide with alarm.

"Bethany," he whispered. Then his lips found hers, again, tentatively at first as he sampled their ripe sweetness. He felt her hands curl into fists against his chest. Then the hands flattened. The warmth of them penetrated his skin and her lips softened beneath his.

Before Bethany could resist Tiger eased her back against the pillows and lay down beside her.

"No, no, please!" Frightened now, she broke away from him and tried to sit up.

"I only want to hold you," Tiger said as he took her into his arms. The golden cloud of her hair brushed his face as he lay back on the bed with her. He kissed her cheek and felt a rush of tenderness that he'd never known before. Taking her face in his hands he gently kissed her closed eyes. "Go to sleep," he whispered, then he drew her down beside him and did not speak again.

She knew he could feel the pounding of her heart and the trembling of her body against his. She tensed, waiting for him to move. But he didn't. He only smoothed her hair back from her face and held her until at last the trembling stopped.

A soft breeze stirred the curtains. Beneath them the boat rocked gently. Bethany closed her eyes. Just for a moment, she told herself, only seconds before she went to sleep.

Chapter 4

Tiger awoke when the first streak of dawn lightened the sky. Bethany lay close to him, her leg against his, her head against his shoulder. He gazed at her slightly parted lips and the shadowy fringe of her eyelashes against her cheeks. He saw the rise and fall of small rounded breasts beneath the thin material of her gown and felt a rush of passion.

Tense with desire Tiger slipped from the bed. He stood for a moment looking down at Bethany. Someday soon we will be lovers, he silently promised her. Then, with a strength he had never known he possessed, Tiger left and quietly closed her door behind him.

He went out on deck. The harbor slept; there were no other boats close to the *Golden Dragon*. He dropped his black silk robe on the teak deck, climbed on the rail, poised, then plunged into the sea. The shock of the water stunned him for a moment, then he began to swim, out toward the South China Sea. He swam hard and fast, trying to ease the throb of desire within him. And when at last it began to ebb he rolled onto his back and swam slowly back toward the boat.

He knew that he would take Bethany with him when he went to Kwantung; it wasn't safe for her in Hong Kong now. But that wasn't the only reason. He thought then of the days and nights that he and Bethany would be on board his boat together and he knew that before this trip was over they would be lovers.

Bethany awoke slowly. Without opening her eyes she felt the breeze on her face and the scent of salt in the air. She felt the motion of the boat under her and her brows came together in a puzzled frown. She opened her eyes to look about her, disoriented until she remembered that she was on Tiger Malone's boat. Then came the other memory, the memory of the dream and the feel of Tiger's arms around her in the darkness of the night.

A flush crept into Bethany's cheeks. Tiger had lain here beside her, the whole length of his body against hers, all through the night. She'd felt the strength of his arms around her when she'd tried to pull away, and the strange mixture of emotions. Panic because she didn't know him, fear, an odd kind of excitement, then a quiet comfort as he gently soothed her.

Tiger Malone. Bethany knew that she would go to China with him. She had no idea how long the trip would take or the danger that might lay ahead. But somewhere deep within her she knew that, because of Hong Kong, her life would never be the same again.

The next few days passed in a flurry of activity. Tiger arranged for his manager to take over for him while he was away. He debated taking on an extra crew member but decided that he and Chang Lu could manage the helm and the navigation and Lee Tung could handle the cooking and other chores.

Fuel was taken on, water tanks were filled, a supply of food laid in. Five days after the attack on the dock the *Golden Dragon* was ready.

The day before they left Bethany phoned the States. When the nursing home answered she asked to speak to her mother. After a moment's hesitation the woman at the other end said, "I'm sorry, Miss Adams, but your mother can't speak. We'd hoped by this time she'd be responding, but I'm afraid there's been no change in her condition."

Bethany's hand tightened on the phone.

"I wish I had better news," the nurse said. There was a moment of hesitation. "I hate to trouble you, Miss Adams, but we're concerned about your mother's bill, with you over there in Hong Kong, I mean."

"The bill is paid until the end of the month," Bethany said. "Today I'm sending you a check for the next three months."

Bethany didn't mention that she'd cashed in her return ticket and that she was sending almost all the money she had. She had no idea how long the trip into China would take, but she had to be sure her mother was taken care of. If the statue was as valuable as Tiger said, she'd never have to worry about money again. *If* they found it. If they didn't she'd have to borrow money from him to get home. Once home she'd sell the house and her car to repay him and take care of her mother's bills.

With the money she had left, Bethany decided to go to Stanley Market to buy a few things for the trip. When she told Tiger that she wanted to go shopping he insisted on sending Chang Lu with her.

"But why?" Bethany protested. "I can take a bus to the market. There's no need to bother Chang."

"I don't want you out alone."

Bethany looked at him and felt a cold knot of fear forming somewhere in her midsection. "You don't think that incident on the dock was just a purse-snatching, do you? Or my room being ransacked. You think it had something to do with the dragon."

Tiger hesitated. He didn't want to frighten her, but on the other hand he wanted her to be aware of any possible danger.

"The statue has a history of violence, Bethany," he said at last. "Warlords have been fighting over it for centuries. The man who wanted it smuggled out was murdered before our fathers could deliver it. I'm not certain that the attack on the dock had anything to do with the dragon, but it might." Tiger paused. "I'm certain someone has been following me for the last two months. I thought at first it had something to do with the gambling club, a disgruntled player who held me responsible for his losses. Now I'm not so sure. Maybe someone wants the dragon just as much as we do."

Tiger's green eyes narrowed in thought. "Maybe someone has been waiting all these years, first for my father, then for me to go after the dragon. You came to Hong Kong and the connection between us was recognized; our fathers together took the dragon, a priceless object of art, and hid it away. Suppose whoever it is who wants the dragon believes that you have come to reclaim it?'' His face was serious. ''I think that is why we were attacked the other night, and why your room was broken into.''

A chill of fear ran down Bethany's spine. Before she could speak Tiger put his hands on her shoulders. In a quiet voice he said, ''I only *think* this, Bethany. I have no proof. But that is why I have decided to take you with me.''

''You're taking me with you?'' She could scarcely believe his words.

''You will be safer with me than you would be here in Hong Kong. We could fly to Canton and go on to my mother's from there, but if someone is following us they will check the airport, that's why I choose to go by boat. When we reach Guantung you will stay with my mother. I know you will be safe there.''

''But—''

''No buts.'' Tigers hands tightened. With a small smile to soften his words, he said, ''I am the captain of this ship. From now until we return to Hong Kong I'm in charge. I want you to understand that, Bethany.''

She looked up at him, ready to do battle. Tiger's expression was firm, but within the firmness she saw tenderness. He meant to rule for as long as they were aboard his yacht, but she knew his autocracy would be tempered by his innate decency, his almost old-world courtliness.

Tiger shook her gently. ''Do you understand?'' he asked.

A slight smile touched the corners of Bethany's lips as she brought her hand up in a salute and said, "Aye, aye, Captain Malone. For as long as we're at sea I'll be your humble..." Her eyebrows rose in question. "Deckhand?"

"I'd much prefer you be my First Mate." His eyes warmed with desire. But only for a moment. Then he let her go and stepping away from her said, "We sail at dawn. You'd better get some sleep."

But it was a long time that night before Bethany went to sleep, and when she did it was to dream of the statue of the golden dragon she'd first seen at Tiger's club in Macao. In her dream the dragon's eyes were as warm with desire as Tiger's had been when he'd looked at her.

Bethany awoke the next morning at the first sound of the motor. Quickly she pulled on her blue jeans and a red-and-white-striped shirt and barefoot ran up on deck. Standing at the rail she looked up to the hills, at the homes and the mountains beyond, watching them grow farther and farther away. When Bethany turned to look out to sea she saw Tiger at the helm, looking every inch a captain in navy-blue trousers and a white T-shirt.

With a half-smothered sigh Bethany looked beyond him at the sea. The sky lightened and the sun came up in a red-gold blaze of color. Bethany felt the teak deck under her bare feet, the roll of the waves, and the winds of the South China Sea blowing the hair back from her face. She took a deep breath of clear salt air. Ahead lay China, ancient and mysterious. And whatever the fates had in store for her.

It took Bethany two days to get her sea legs. For the first day she took pills to prevent seasickness but when there was no sign of queasiness she stopped taking them. Lee Tung was a fantastic cook and for the first time since her mother's illness and her father's death, Bethany really began to enjoy food. She had a glow of color in her face from the fresh sea air and the sun and felt better than she'd ever felt in her life.

Tiger and Chang Lu took turns at the helm. Although Tiger spent much of the day working on the cruiser, he always managed to be free to enjoy an evening cocktail and dinner with Bethany after the anchor was lowered and the boat moored for the night near one of the smaller islands that lay between Hong Kong and Lantao Island.

This was the loveliest part of day for Bethany, this quiet time alone with Tiger, sitting in lounge chairs watching the sunset, listening to music from the stereo in the salon. It was a time of intense awareness of the beauty that surrounded her and of this man, so different from any man she'd ever known. It seemed to Bethany that they were alone in the world, far from all of the trappings and responsibilities of civilization, two people afloat on the sea as the sun cast jeweled colors on the horizon and slowly disappeared. At that precise moment, when the last rays of the sun turned Tiger's skin a golden bronze, Bethany felt an almost overpowering desire to touch him. There were mystery and beauty in his face, and a sensuality that threatened to undo her.

At twenty-four Bethany was quite proper, although not totally innocent. But never in her life had she felt about a man what she was beginning to feel for Tiger

Malone. To compensate for her feelings she tried desperately to keep herself coolly remote. She was friendly, but not too friendly. Pleasant, but not too pleasant. Each night when she closed the door of her cabin she stood for a moment, alone in the dark, breathing a sigh of relief—and of regret—that another day had passed without Tiger making a move toward her.

It was late afternoon and Bethany lay prone on the aft deck, the straps of her bikini untied so that her back would tan evenly. Tiger was at the helm, waiting for Chang to take over, and Lee was in the galley preparing dinner. She was alone, feeling the hot rays of the sun beating down on her body, melting her bones, lost in a lovely haze between sleep and consciousness.

She didn't hear his footsteps, but suddenly she became aware of a shadow across her body, and looked up to see Tiger standing over her. Her gaze skimmed up long straight legs to his narrow hips and flat stomach. He wore nothing but a sleek black pair of bikini trunks.

Before Bethany could speak he dropped to the mat next to her, saying, "You're going to burn."

"I forgot to buy suntan lotion." She started to turn, then remembered she'd untied the straps that would keep her top in place. Quickly she lay down again and brought her arms close to her body.

"I have some jasmine oil. Let me rub it on your back."

"No, that's all right. I—"

But it was too late. She felt the warm oil trickle onto her skin, then his hands, strong and smooth on her legs, soothing, caressing.

"Close your eyes," Tiger said. "Relax."

Relax! Every muscle in Bethany's body tensed. She could feel his thigh pressing against her hip, and his hand seemed to burn right down through her bones.

One hand rested on her calf. "You have the most beautiful legs I have ever seen," he said. The hand moved down and she felt his fingers circle her ankle before it began to move up again. He paused, then shifted onto his knees so that he could rub both her legs at the same time. She wanted to stop him, but his hands were so warm as they kneaded and warmed their way up to her thighs. Bethany closed her eyes and sighed. This felt so good, so... A shock ran through Bethany's body as Tiger's thumb caressed the inside of her thighs, but before she could speak Tiger said, "Your skin is so tender here, so soft and pale. I must put the oil here or you'll burn."

Bethany buried her face in the mat. His touch was magic, arousing feelings she'd never even dreamed of. By the time he moved once more to put lotion on her back she felt as though her body was on fire. He slipped the blue bikini bottom an inch lower and said, "What lovely dimples."

Bethany struggled to sit up, and clasping the top of her suit close to her breasts said, "Tiger, please."

"I'm sorry. I was teasing." Gently Tiger pushed her down to the mat. He drizzled the oil of Jasmine onto her back and began to rub it into her skin.

His hands were warm, and again, in spite of herself, Bethany began to relax. She felt the gentle roll of the boat beneath her body, the sun beating down, and Tiger's hands moving up and down her back, lulling her to a state of drifting somnolence.

Then Tiger rolled her over and cast aside the top that covered her breasts. Bethany's eyes opened. Through the blaze of the sun she looked up at him. She started to speak, tried to cover her nakedness, but he said, "No, Bethany," and his oil slick hands cupped and caressed her breasts.

She heard him catch his breath in his throat, saw through eyes half blinded by the sun the passion in his face.

"Someone will see," Bethany whispered.

"Lee Tung is in the galley, Chang is at the helm. We are alone, Bethany, and I have wanted to touch you like this from the moment you walked into my office."

Tiger brushed the windblown hair back off her face. "My lovely Bethany," he said. "I have waited so long." He ran his thumb across her lips. "Do you know how much I wanted you that first night on the yacht? Do you know how much my body ached with the need of you?" He leaned to kiss her lips and with a smile said, "You smell like sunlight and jasmine."

"Tiger?" His name trembled on her lips.

"Close your eyes," he said. "What there is between us can wait . . . for a little while."

Then he poured more oil of jasmine on her breasts and slowly and leisurely rubbed it into her skin.

That evening, after the cruiser had been moored at the lee side of a small, uninhabited island, they had dinner of fresh fish and a cool green salad on the aft deck. Chang Lu poured their wine and after he had placed it in the ice bucket beside the table he said, "If you do not need anything else I will retire."

"Thank you, Chang. I won't need you any more this evening. Just check the mooring lines before you turn in." When the man had left Tiger looked at Bethany. "You look lovely tonight," he said. "But your nose is burned."

"I don't see how that could be. I thought you covered every inch of me... I mean... I..." Hot color flooded Bethany's face as she looked down at her plate. She wished she'd worn jeans and a high-necked shirt instead of the short sky-blue, cotton T-dress that slipped off one shoulder. Because she was sunburned—that's what she'd told herself—she hadn't worn a bra. Now Bethany crossed her bare legs under the table and tried to think of something to say.

An old Barry Manilow tune drifted out from the salon to break the silence. The sky darkened and the moon rose, big and fat and yellow, from behind the island hills.

Bethany took the last bite of her fish and put down her fork.

"More champagne?" As Tiger refilled her glass his fingers brushed her. He hesitated after replacing the bottle, then curled his fingers around hers. "Bethany?"

She looked into his slightly tilted green eyes. For a moment it seemed to her that there was no air to breathe. "Yes, Tiger," she said in affirmation to his unspoken question.

Chapter 5

Black and gold were the colors of Tiger's stateroom. When he led Bethany in and closed the door he stood for a moment with his arms around her, breathing in the scent of her clean hair and the delicate trace of perfume. Her body was warm and soft against his. He could feel the press of her breasts against his chest and the slight trembling of the hands that crept up around his neck.

In a few moments Bethany would be his, but now he would savor the waiting. He cupped her face with his hands and tilted it up so that he could look at her. Tiger saw a look of shyness in her gray eyes, shadowed by fear of the unknown, of him, and of this new aspect of their relationship. Then he gently kissed her, not pressing until her lips softened beneath his. When her lips parted he caressed them with his tongue, then slid into the moistness of her mouth. Her tongue danced to meet his and he felt a surge of joy flash through his body, knowing that she wanted this as much as he did.

She'd never known a kiss like this, had never felt such a kindling passion. When Tiger let her go she swayed toward him and he kissed her again, kissed her with such fire and warmth that for a moment she was afraid. But when he touched her breasts through the fabric of the T-dress her fear was forgotten in the surge of feeling that coursed through her body.

Tiger took her hand and led her to his bed. He threw back the black silk spread and turned to face her. Without a word Bethany raised her arms so that he could remove her dress. When he had taken it off he looked at her for a moment. Then he moved to the porthole to pull back the curtains so that moonlight flooded the room.

"You're beautiful." Tiger's voice was so low Bethany could barely hear him. He took a step toward her, then stopped and hastily removed his clothes.

His body, in the path of golden moonlight, was more beautiful than Bethany could have imagined. Bethany's heart pounded as he slowly came toward her. Without a word Tiger picked her up and laid her on the bed. For a moment he only looked at her, then he slipped off her sandals and slid the blue lace panties down over her hips.

Bethany brought one hand up to touch his shoulder, as though to reassure herself. Tiger took her hand and kissed it. Then he lay down beside her and gathered her in his arms.

The shock of him against her naked body sent a shiver of excitement through Bethany. The feel of his lips on hers both frightened and thrilled her. He kissed her closed eyelids, traveled down her throat, then back up to her ears, nibbling, caressing, sending electric waves of pleasure through Bethany's body. He touched her breasts and she couldn't smother the moan that escaped her lips.

"I knew this afternoon that I would kiss your breasts tonight," Tiger said against her skin. His hands slid around her back, forcing her breasts upward. She heard his indrawn breath as he gazed at her intently. Slowly, with loving care, he bestowed butterfly kisses on her skin. When Bethany sighed and her fingers curled in the blackness of his hair, he flicked one peaked tip with his tongue, then took it into his mouth to tease and suckle.

It was a sweet torture that left Bethany whispering helplessly as she stroked Tiger's shoulders. Wave after wave of ecstasy flooded her body and an urgency that was almost past bearing took possession of her. She murmured his name as he continued to caress her.

Gently he soothed her throbbing breasts and came up to kiss her parted lips. "Now we will be one person," he said. He rose above her. "Look at me, Bethany. Look at me when our bodies join."

Before she could speak he entered her and the feel of him inside her was like nothing she had ever experienced before. She cried out. Her heart beat in rhythm to his thrusts as he moved deeper and ever deeper. She welcomed the weight of his body covering hers, rejoiced in his strength as she moved with him. The need to be closer and still closer grew as Bethany lifted her body to his. Small cries of delight whispered through her trembling lips as her hands tightened on his shoulders. Fire seared her loins as she gave herself up to the urgency of Tiger's demands and to the demands of her own body.

"Bethany, my love," he whispered as his body moved against hers, then quickened. It was more than Bethany could bear. Her fingers tangled and tightened in Tiger's hair. She tasted his shoulder, not even aware that her teeth were scraping his skin, and lifted her body to his in one final, glorious moment of passion.

With a cry Tiger sought Bethany's mouth, and united as one, they climbed the heights of love and fell slowly back to reality in the warm comfort of each other's arms.

Heart beating wildly against heart, Tiger rained kisses on her face. He told her in Chinese and in English how beautiful she was, how wonderful it had been for him.

Bethany's eyes were luminous in the aftermath of love as she caressed Tiger's back. As they lay side by side Tiger took Bethany's hand and brought it to his lips. "I hope I have made you as happy as you have made me." He looked at her. His face was calm, his green eyes serious. "I think I have known from the first moment I saw you what would be between us, Bethany. But I did not expect...I did not dare to dream that it would be so much."

Dazed by happiness that was mingled with an edge of apprehension, Bethany looked at Tiger in wonder. How is it possible, she thought, that something like this could happen so fast? I don't even know him. He's different from all that I'm familiar with, yet with him I've experienced a joy I never thought possible.

She closed her eyes and rested her face against his chest. Tiger Malone. She repeated his name like a litany before she fell into a deep sleep.

The next morning they dived off the bow of the *Golden Dragon*. There was the threat of rain in the air as they swam leisurely, side by side, around the lee side of the island. When they were out of sight of the boat and their feet touched bottom, Tiger pulled Bethany close and gave her a salty kiss.

"You are even more beautiful this morning than you were last night," he told her. "Your eyes are shining, your face has a look of pleasure."

"Because of you," Bethany said. "Because of the way you make me feel." She smoothed the sleek black hair off his forehead. "I didn't want all this to happen, Tiger. But I think I, too, knew that it was inevitable."

"As inevitable as love." His hands caressed her back, then gently crept around to push the bikini top aside so that he could touch her breasts.

Bethany shivered in the early morning air. Head back, long blond hair streaming over her shoulders, she yielded herself up to the lips so tenderly caressing her. When Tiger picked her up and carried her toward the shore she buried her face in his throat, shivering with the anticipation of what was to come.

He laid her down under the shelter of a sea grape tree. For a moment he looked down at her, then knelt to slide the bikini bottom down over her hips.

Bethany heard the soft patter of raindrops on the overhang of leaves as she held up her arms to receive

Tiger. He kissed her. "You taste of the sea," he said with a smile. "I must see if you taste this way all over."

"Tiger...?" Then his mouth found her breasts and there was no need for words.

When he came up over her she received him with a glad cry, embracing him with her arms and her legs as she lifted herself to him. She was unmindful of the rain or the hard-packed sand beneath her body. All that mattered was the feel of him inside her, the lovely slowness of his movements, the look on his face. She reached up to touch him, to trace the high cheekbones, the line of his jaw, the curve of his mouth.

"Bethany!" Tiger's green eyes closed, his face tensed, his movements quickened as he carried Bethany higher and higher into a vortex of emotion that left her throbbing with need. She cried his name. He took her cry into his mouth; his body tightened and exploded.

They lay on the sand, still heedless of the rain and of the rising wind, until Tiger said, "There's a storm coming, we have to get back." He helped Bethany up and led her down to the beach. Then he kissed her and smoothed the rain-wet hair back from her face. "I wish you could see the way you look," he said. "Your eyes are beautiful and your lips are swollen from my kisses." He ran his hands down her shoulders to the rise of her breasts, circled her waist and smoothed the curve of her hips. "I'd like to keep you naked forever," he said, "but we must dress and swim back to the *Dragon*."

Tiger hesitated. His hands crept around to cup her bare buttocks. "But first..." He dropped to his knees on the sand. Still cupping Bethany he urged her closer and rested his face against her before he began to trail a line of kisses across her stomach, down and down. A tickle of flame licked at her insides.

"No," Bethany whispered. "Tiger, no, please." She tried to move away but his hands tightened and he pressed her closer. He nipped the inside of her thighs, then quickly, before Bethany could stop him, found the burning heart of her.

She cried out and tried to break free. But the hands that held her were implacable, the lips that caressed her immovable.

The rain was falling harder now, but still Tiger held her, held her and kissed her in that secret place until her fingers tightened in his rain-wet hair. Until her legs trembled and threatened to give way and she cried his name into the wind, shattered and weeping with an ecstasy she'd never known before.

When finally he held her in his arms he said, "There has never been anyone like you, Bethany. There will never be anyone like you." He tilted her chin and looked directly into her wide gray eyes. "I am not a promiscuous man, but there have been other women in my life. But there have been none with whom I have felt what I feel for you." He smoothed her hair back from her face once more. "We'll talk about this later; now we really must leave." Then he took her hand and led her into the water.

The sea was rough, even here in the lee of the island. Bethany was a strong swimmer, but Tiger cursed himself for having endangered her this way. They shouldn't have lingered on the island when the rain began, but when he had touched her, when he had kissed her, the heat of his desire had driven every sen-

sible thought from his head. He looked at her, so close
beside him, white arms cutting through the waves, the
golden hair streaming out behind her. What am I
doing? he thought. Why does this woman make the
blood sing in my veins and make me forget that I am
a sensible man who does not take unnecessary risks?
This was foolhardy; I've put her in danger. If anything happens to her I'll never forgive myself.

Then through the roll of the waves Bethany flashed
him a smile, and it seemed to Tiger as though his heart
stood still.

Chang was waiting for them. As soon as he spotted
them he lowered the ladder and reaching a hand down
to Bethany, helped her aboard.

"I've been watching for you," he said to Tiger. "In
another five minutes I would have lowered the raft and
come out looking for you."

"We were waiting for the rain to stop," Tiger lied.
He took one of the robes Chang offered and wrapped
it around Bethany. "Take a warm shower," he said.
"We'll stay here until the storm passes."

"No, we can't wait." Chang's face was serious. "I
looked for you through the binoculars a short while
ago and I saw a boat heading in our direction. After
what you told me..." He glanced at Bethany and
hesitated.

"It's all right, you may speak in front of Bethany."
Tiger put an arm around her shoulders. "Go below,"
he said. And to Chang he said, "Raise the anchor,
we're heading out."

Bethany stared at Tiger, lower lip caught between
her teeth, feeling a chill through her body that had
nothing to do with the wind or the rain. As she started

toward the stairs Tiger ran forward to the wheel-house.

By the time Bethany had showered and dressed in jeans and a long-sleeved pullover, the sky had darkened to a sullen gray. Rain slashed against the port-hole, the wind was stronger and thunder rumbled in the distance. She bent to pull on her sneakers, hanging on to the headboard to stop herself from falling. Like a drunkard she staggered across the cabin to the door, lurching with the roll of the ship. Out in the companionway she grasped the railing to keep herself steady, then headed for the ladder leading to the deck.

The wind hit Bethany hard, almost knocking her off her feet. She clutched a rail for support, trying to see through the driving rain. Tiger was in the wheel-house, bare feet braced against the terrible swaying of the ship as giant gray waves splashed over the *Dragon*'s sides threatening to swamp her.

Bethany bent her head against the force of the wind and started toward the wheelhouse just as Chang reached her. "Go back," he said. "Stay in your state-room until this is over."

"I want to help." Bethany raised her voice, trying to be heard above the roar of the wind.

Chang shook his head. "This is a typhoon," he said. "Go below."

Half falling, half staggering, Bethany groped her way back to her cabin. The door slammed behind her as she zigzagged to the bed. It seemed impossible that the cruiser could withstand the force of the storm. She'd seen the high waves, the deep troughs of gray water lashing over the decks as the *Dragon* plunged down, hesitated for a heart-stopping moment, then roller-coastered back up. She'd almost forgotten about the boat that Chang said might be following them. That seemed of little importance now. All that mattered was making it safely through the storm.

Hours passed. Bethany sat up in bed, her back braced against the bulkhead. Too frightened to be seasick, all she could do was hang on and pray that the *Dragon* would weather the storm. By late afternoon she couldn't stand the solitude any longer. She put on a sweater, covered her hair with a scarf, and fought her way to the galley. Lee Tung, his round face wrinkled in a worried frown, short legs hooked around the rungs of a fastened-down chair, looked up. "You hungry, missy?" he asked.

Bethany shook her head. "But I'd like a cup of coffee."

"There is a fresh pot in the oven." Seeing her puzzled frown he said, "It would not stay on top of stove so I put it in the oven."

Bethany braced herself against the wall as she opened the oven door. She looked at the stove, not sure how to light it. With a sigh Lee Tung unwrapped his feet and lunged for the stove. Quickly he lit it, then angled back to his chair.

When the coffee was hot Bethany poured a cup for herself. Then she looked inside the refrigerator and finding wrapped ham and cheese, took them out and made six fat sandwiches. She filled a thermos with coffee, and added a good-sized dollop of brandy, then put everything into a canvas bag she found under the counter. Putting the bag over her shoulder and taking a deep breath she bade goodbye to the frightened cook and aimed for the door.

The force of the wind was even stronger now. It flung the door out of Bethany's hand and threw her back against the boat. Quickly she grabbed a safety line. She managed to close the door, then began her slow struggle toward the wheelhouse. Waves lashed over the *Dragon*'s bow. Rain blinded her and her hand tightened on the line.

As she grew closer the door of the wheelhouse was flung open and Tiger pulled her inside.

"You were told to stay in your stateroom," he said. He looked tired. His face was drawn and grim.

"I couldn't stand it in there another minute. Besides you had to have something to eat, and from the look of Lee Tung I doubt that he's fixed anything for you."

"Lee does not like storms," Chang said from the helm. "Each time we go through one he vows he will never set foot on a ship again."

"I made some sandwiches," Bethany said. "You've got to eat something."

Tiger looked at her approvingly. "You're wet," he said. He helped her remove the sweater and handed her a towel and a windbreaker. "Dry off, then put this jacket on." To Chang he said, "I'll take the wheel now; you have a sandwich and a cup of coffee."

"No, you eat first. I will stay until you finish."

Tiger took Bethany's arm, and bracing himself, led her to the curved seat at the side of the wheelhouse. When she handed him a sandwich he took a bite and said, "I didn't realize how hungry I was." He looked at her. "Are you all right? I was afraid you would be sick."

"I was much too frightened to be sick," she said with a smile.

"Was? Does that mean you are no longer afraid?"

"Not here with you, Tiger." Bethany touched his hand. "You look so tired."

He ran a hand across his face. "I am, and so is Chang. After he eats I'll make him go and rest." He took another bite of the sandwich. "As soon as we left the island I used the radio. What we are in now is the tag end of a typhoon by the name of Angelica." His lips quirked. "But Angelica is no angel. This is one of the worst storms I've ever been in. I've never seen anything like it before."

"How long will it last?"

Tiger glanced at his watch. "It's after six. The storm has been raging for almost eight hours. It can go on far into the night. Or into the morning. We just have to ride her out."

"Can we?" She took a deep breath. "I don't see how a boat can take a beating like this and still stay afloat."

"The *Dragon*'s a seaworthy craft. She'll weather this." Tiger took a second sandwich and drank his coffee. Then he leaned back against the curved seat, and with his arm around Bethany, closed his eyes.

Bethany let him rest. Trying not to disturb him, she managed to hand the coffee and sandwiches to Chang, then sat close to Tiger. After a while she too closed her eyes and slept.

She awoke to silence. The wind had stopped. The sea was still rough but not as bad as it had been. Beside her Tiger stirred and opened his eyes. "It's over,"

Bethany said as she turned to him. "Tiger, the storm's over."

He sat up straighter and flexed his shoulders. "No, Bethany, this is the eye of the storm." He stood up. "How long have we been in it?" he asked Chang.

"Twenty minutes."

Tiger glanced at his watch. "It's nine-fifteen. Why don't you check for any damage now, while there is the opportunity? Report back to me, then get some rest. I have a feeling it's going to be a long night."

"But there's no wind," Bethany said. "Aren't we all right now?"

Tiger shook his head. "A typhoon is shaped something like a donut. One section of it comes, then there is the hole—the eye—where nothing happens. After that there is the other side of the storm."

"How long will the eye last?"

"Anywhere from half an hour to an hour, or even a little longer. But when it passes the storm will begin again, probably even worse than before." Tiger looked down at her. "Perhaps you would be better off in your cabin," he said.

"No." Bethany shook her head. "I want to stay with you."

"It may be a long night."

"That doesn't matter."

Tiger's green eyes appraised her. "Very well," he said, "you may stay."

He was right, it was a long night. The wind rose to a furious pitch. Each wave that crashed over the *Dragon*'s bow seemed even more menacing than the last. Down, down, down, the cruiser plunged and each time Bethany held her breath, praying, tensing her

shoulders as though by sheer willpower she could
bring the boat out of the trough that appeared to be
carrying her down into the depths of the sea.

Tiger fought the wheel, his face grimly determined
as he brought the boat back up out of the waves.

Bethany stood beside him through the long dark
night, her feet braced, hands curled around a strut as
she tried to keep her balance. At last, just before
dawn, the wind lessened and Tiger's grip on the wheel
relaxed. With a tired smile he looked at her and said,
"We've made it, Bethany. We'll be all right now."

A few minutes later Chang came into the wheelhouse, full of apologies for having slept so long. "I'll
take the wheel," he said to Tiger.

"How is the *Dragon*? Was there any damage?"

"Only to the salon. The glass in one of the portholes shattered and there's water damage. Lee is
mopping up. Also he has managed to prepare something for you and Miss Bethany to eat. Then you must
rest, Tiger."

"I will." Tiger stepped aside to give Chang the
wheel. "Is there any sign of the boat that was following us?"

Chang shook his head. "I searched the sea with
binoculars. I could see no one. I've told Lee that as
soon as he serves you he's to keep watch. But don't
worry, Tiger, I'm sure we lost them in the storm."

"You're probably right." Tiger took Bethany's arm.
"I'll relieve you at noon," he told Chang as he guided
her out of the pilothouse.

They went down to the galley where they breakfasted on bacon and eggs, hot rolls and coffee. When

they were finished Tiger said, "Let's get some sleep now." His hand closed over Bethany's.

They left the galley and headed for the companionway. Tiger led Bethany to the door of his cabin. "I must sleep," he said, "but I want to sleep with you beside me."

Bethany looked up at him for a moment. Then she rested her hand against the side of her face. "I want to sleep beside you, too," she said softly.

He brushed his lips against hers, and together they went into the cabin.

Chapter 6

The sea was calm, the air still when Bethany awoke late the next morning. Tiger lay on his side, breathing deeply, the sheet covering him from the waist down. A day's growth of beard shadowed his face and there were patches of fatigue under his eyes. He had fallen into bed exhausted from his long hours at the helm, reached for Bethany's hand, and with a sigh had closed his eyes and gone to sleep.

Bethany looked at him and caught her breath. Tiger was handsome in a way that no other man in the world was handsome. His features were classic, his skin clear and smooth. But those weren't the things that made him so special, so different. There was a mystery about him, a fathomless depth in the emerald-green eyes, that slight Eurasian look, the sensual fullness of his lips that stirred her as no one ever had.

Almost from the moment Bethany met Tiger, everything had been cloaked in adventure. She hadn't had time to think or to rationalize. Tiger Malone lived in a different world than she did, a world of exotic flavors and excitement. She was a small town girl. Her area of experience had been limited to Tiffin and the four years she'd spent at Ohio Wesleyan, a university close enough to Tiffin that she'd been able to go home every weekend. Her only short romance had been with a young man from her hometown, and her only job had been at her father's flying school.

She and Tiger Malone had nothing in common. The whole shape of their lives was different. They had different responsibilities. Her mother was ill; she would return to Tiffin as soon as she and Tiger found and sold the golden dragon.

I shouldn't have let myself fall in love with him, she thought as she looked at his sleeping face. But now it's too late, and I don't know what I'm going to do.

Tiger opened his eyes and looked at her. "What is it?" he asked in a sleepy voice. "Why are you sad?"

Bethany smoothed the dark hair off his forehead. "I'm not sad," she lied. "Just tired."

"Then come and rest in my arms." Tiger raised himself on one elbow to see the clock. "I must relieve Chang at twelve, that gives us thirty minutes." He kissed her. "What can we do in thirty minutes?"

"Shower and dress and have breakfast." Bethany ran her hand across his chest, entwining her fingers in the thatch of black chest hair. Slowly her fingers moved downward.

The green eyes widened, the nostrils flared, but Tiger didn't move as Bethany followed the line of curly black hair below his navel. She heard the sharp intake of his breath and felt the fire within her own body as her hand descended even further. Lightly, softly, she caressed him. He closed his eyes and sighed with pleasure at her touch, wondering if she knew how much this pleased him, how the touch of her fingers against his flesh sent hot licks of flame through every part of his body.

With a smothered moan Tiger closed his eyes, enduring this sweet torture, making himself wait because he knew that in a moment he would possess her. Soon. Very soon. His body quivered with need. With a groan his hand closed on Bethany's wrist and he rolled her beneath him.

"My sea witch," he whispered as he began to move against her, reveling in her sweet moistness, thrilling to the sigh of pleasure that escaped her lips. He wanted her now, wanted her to cry his name in the silence of the room and tell him that she loved him.

But it was Tiger who cried out. With frantic hands he cupped her buttocks to bring her closer. He kissed her lips and told her how wonderful she was, how beautiful.

Bethany was helpless against the strength of his hands, the force of his thrusts, lost in the power and the pleasure, as she gave herself up to it with small cries of joy.

Oh, how she loved the feel of Tiger's body against hers, the pressure of the hands that urged her closer. Bethany felt enveloped by him. Everything else was forgotten. All of the realities that only a moment before had seemed so important faded away. She kissed the side of his face, relishing the rough scrape of his beard against her tender skin. Hungrily she found his lips, nipping their fullness before her tongue sought his in a silken duel. She heard the rasp of his breath against her throat and felt a thrill of excitement at her daring because she knew she was pleasing him.

Gripping her hips Tiger brought her even closer. He found her breasts and his teeth tightened on one swollen bud. He flicked hard with his tongue, then took the tip between his teeth to tease and tug.

Bethany was lost in a whirlwind of desire; beyond thought or reason, carried high on the crest of an ecstasy too great to bear as Tiger whispered her name and together, clinging lest they fall off the world, they climbed to that highest peak of existence where only lovers venture.

When their breathing slowed Tiger gently brushed the damp hair from Bethany's forehead. Wordlessly he kissed her, again and again, soft kisses across her cheeks, her nose, her eyelids. His hands caressed her swollen breasts, then moved to the line of her back, soothing, calming. At last with a sigh he let her go.

"I have to relieve Chang," he said. "Do you mind if I shower first?" He smiled. "I'd like to shower with you but I know that if I do it will begin again." He took a strand of her golden hair and wrapped it around his finger as he looked at her. His face was serious, his eyes puzzled. "I don't know what it is you do to me, Bethany. What we shared a few moments ago should have been enough to last me for a while. But when I look at you I want you again and that frightens me. I wonder if there will ever be enough time for me to have all I want to have of you." He kissed her lips, then quickly, before he changed his mind, went in to shower.

Bethany closed her eyes. There won't be enough time, my love, she thought. When this China adventure is over I'll say goodbye to you and to this wondrous magic that we've shared. Tears welled in her eyes as she turned her face into the pillow, wondering how she'd ever bear to leave him.

The next few days passed without incident. They put in to another of the small islands for fuel and supplies. That night they moored the *Dragon* in the island's marina at a dock some distance from the other boats. Lee Tung had relatives on the island so Tiger told both Lee and Chang to spend the night ashore.

Since the cyclone all four of them had taken turns standing watch. Either Tiger or Bethany searched the sea with binoculars during the day. At night when they moored the watch was divided between Chang and Lee.

The morning after the cyclone, on Tiger's insistence, Bethany had moved her things into his cabin. She protested at first, worried about what the crew might think, but Tiger hadn't listened to her arguments. They were together now and they would be together until the end of their voyage.

That night in port, when they were alone, Tiger fixed two tall gin and tonics and brought them out on deck. He looked at Bethany approvingly as he handed her her drink. The sun had tanned her skin a deep golden color, and tonight, dressed in a white summer dress that just skimmed her shoulders, with her blond hair brushed loose, she looked so beautiful that she took his breath away.

Just for a moment his hand rested on one slender ankle, then he said, "Lee left a salad and dessert in the refrigerator. We'll eat later if you don't mind waiting a bit."

"No, it's lovely here. I don't think I've ever seen such a glorious sky."

Tiger sank down on the lounge beside her. He reached for Bethany's hand as together they watched the sky change from gold to salmon pink to vermilion and slowly darken. From the shore came the clamorous chorus of night birds coming in to roost. Gulls circled and glided low. The boat moved gently on the evening tide.

"There's never been a night like this before." Bethany's voice was hushed. "I'll remember it for as long as I live, Tiger."

"As I will remember the way you look in this moment with the last rays of the sun on your face." Tiger brought her hand to his lips. "My sweet Bethany," he said. "How did I manage before you came into my life?"

He put his arm around her and for a long time they didn't speak. When the sky grew dark they went into the galley and carried the plates that Lee had fixed for them back out on deck. They had just finished when Tiger noticed approaching lights and with a frown said, "That boat is coming in too fast. I hope the skipper knows what he's doing." He put his plate down and went to stand by the rail, muttering, "If he doesn't slow down he's going to tear up half the dock."

But the boat did slow down, just at the last minute, narrowly missing the small schooner next to it as it glided in.

"Bloody fool," Tiger murmured as he watched the boat tie up. Two men sprinted to the dock, growled something to a marina worker who was apparently telling them they'd come in too fast, and hurried ashore.

"They'll probably be drunk by midnight," Tiger said. "I think we will be wise to leave before they do in the morning so we don't get rammed." He looked at Bethany. "Ready to go below?"

"Just a few more minutes; it's such a beautiful night." She went to stand beside Tiger, and when he put his arm around her she said, "It's so quiet now, even the night birds are asleep." She looked up at him. "I'm glad we made this trip, Tiger. Even if we don't find the dragon I won't be sorry that I came."

"Nor will I, Bethany. The dragon brought us together. For me that is treasure enough." He brushed a kiss alongside her temple. In a few minutes they would go below. He would pull the curtains over the portholes and by the light of the bedside lamp he would take off Bethany's white dress and lay her down on the black silk spread. Slowly he'd slide her panties down over her hips and—

"Ahoy the *Dragon*!" Chang called in Chinese.

Tiger looked startled as he hurried to the ladder, Bethany only a step behind him.

Chang scrambled quickly up to the deck. "I saw the boat that just came in," he said, trying to catch his breath. "I'm sure it is the same boat, Tiger, the one I saw through the binoculars just before the storm. I followed the two men that came running off the dock. They asked the harbormaster if the *Dragon* was here.''

"Damn!" Tiger caught his lower lip between his teeth. "We've got to get out of here. What about Lee? Did you tell him?''

Chang shook his head. "No, I came directly here.''

"Then we sail without him.''

"But you can't leave him here!" Bethany protested.

"We don't have any choice. We'll pick him up on the way back.'' Tiger started toward the wheelhouse. "Cast off, Chang.''

"Yes sir.'' Chang sprinted back down the ladder to the dock. A voice rang out a Chinese command to stop as he ran to the mooring lines. Footsteps pounded down the dock toward them.

"Hurry!'' Tiger called from the wheelhouse as the engine started.

Chang raced to the other mooring rope. A shot rang out. Bethany screamed and ran to the ladder. "Chang,'' she cried. "Chang, hurry!''

He flung the rope off the stanchion. Another shot cracked. Chang cried out and slammed against the side of the boat.

Two men raced toward him. Bethany saw them through the darkness as she started down the ladder to Chang. Behind her Tiger cried, "Bethany, no! Get back!''

Chang staggered toward her.

More shots were fired, this time from the *Dragon* just as Bethany reached Chang. She put an arm around his waist and propelled him toward the ladder, then up. Another shot rang out. She flattened herself against the ladder. A hand fastened itself around her ankle, she screamed as she tried to kick herself free, and turned to look into the face of the man who'd assaulted her on the dock in Hong Kong.

Suddenly Tiger jumped past her onto the dock. She saw the flash of a knife, and turned her head as the man who'd grabbed her staggered back.

More shouts went up along the dock as Tiger backed toward Bethany. She heard the roar of the engine and knew that Chang must be in the wheelhouse. Tiger turned, shoved Bethany up the ladder, and bounded onto the deck beside her. "Stay low," he shouted as he sprinted toward the wheelhouse.

His voice was followed by another burst of firing and Bethany dropped to the deck. The *Dragon* moved away from the dock, angled around other boats, and headed back to sea. Bethany lay flat against the teak deck, waiting until the last shot had been fired. Then she got up and ran to the wheelhouse. Blood spattered the floor; Chang slumped on the padded circular seat.

"There's a first-aid kit in the galley," Tiger said. "Take care of Chang, I can't leave the helm."

"Yes, all right." There were a lot of questions Bethany wanted to ask, but she knew this wasn't the time to ask them. She found the first-aid kit and hurried back to the wheelhouse.

Chang's right pant leg was soaked with blood. Bethany eased him back against the cushions, then cut the material away so she could see the wound. The Red Cross course she'd taken in college hadn't prepared her for this. She took a deep breath and quickly sponged the blood away from the wound.

"How is he?" Tiger asked from the helm. "Did the bullet shatter anything?"

"No, I . . . I don't think so. It looks like the bullet went through the fleshy part of his thigh, in and out. I don't think it hit bone."

"Can you handle it?"

Bethany looked at Chang and summoned a smile that she hoped was more confident than she felt as she said, "Yes, it's a superficial wound."

As quickly and as efficiently as she could, Bethany cleaned the wound, applied an antiseptic, then bandaged Chang's leg. When that was done she gave him two aspirin and one of the antibiotics she found in the kit and covered him with a blanket.

"Try to sleep," Tiger told Chang.

"I will be all right in a little while," Chang said as he closed his eyes. His face contorted with pain and he turned toward the bulkhead.

"Was the leg bad?" Tiger asked in a low voice when Bethany came to stand beside him at the wheel.

"I'm not sure. I don't think so, but my knowledge of bullet wounds is pretty limited." She looked at him, then after a moment's hesitation said, "I recognized one of the men, Tiger. He was the same man who tried to grab my purse on the dock in Hong Kong."

His dark brows came together in a scowl. "Then they've made the connection between us. They know we're after the dragon."

"But who are they?"

"I wish I knew. Perhaps they have some connection with the warlord our fathers smuggled the dragon out for forty years ago." He checked the heading and turned the wheel a little to the right. "Whoever they are, I don't think we've heard the last of them."

Bethany stepped closer to him. "Can we outrun them?"

"Yes, with any luck. We'll stay on this course tonight. By daylight, if we're lucky, we will find a cluster of islands. If we can slip in among the islands we stand a good chance of eluding them." Tiger put his arm around her and squeezed her close. When he let her go he said, "I'd like you to go aft and stand watch, Bethany. If you see lights behind us come and tell me immediately."

Bethany nodded. She left Tiger, and after she had checked to see that Chang was asleep, she went aft. Now that the emergency was over she felt weary. She yawned and went to stand by the rail because she knew she would fall asleep if she sat down. The lights from shore had already faded. There were only stars and a thin slice of moon that drifted in and out of the clouds to guide them.

So much had happened to her in such a short space of time that even now all of this seemed like a dream. She'd come to Hong Kong a little over two weeks before. In that short time her life had changed. She'd fallen in love with a man named Tiger Malone. She'd been mugged, robbed, shot at, and she'd survived a typhoon. Bethany stared out at the white wake of the sea. Never before had she experienced even the slightest hint of danger. It seemed so incredible to be standing here, thousands of miles from home, looking for the lights of a boat that was chasing them. Two weeks ago she hadn't known the difference between forward and aft, port and starboard. She'd known what a galley was, but she'd never been in one. And love was something she'd read about in books, but she'd never been in love.

Until now. Until Tiger.

Through the long night Bethany stayed at her post. At dawn she went up to the wheelhouse. "There's nothing on the horizon," she told Tiger.

Chang was sitting up. She gave him two more aspirin and another antibiotic when he said his leg hurt.

"I'll make some coffee," she said, "and whatever I can find for breakfast." She grinned at both Tiger and Chang. "I'm afraid you're stuck with my cooking until we reach China," she told them. "Just don't expect chateaubriand and chocolate mousse."

"With you a cheese sandwich will taste like gourmet cooking," Tiger said. He smiled as Bethany saluted him and left the pilothouse.

"She is a remarkable woman," Chang said. "It was not my place to say, but when we began this journey I thought you were wrong to bring her. I thought she would be trouble, that she would complain at the first sign of hardship. But she did not. Last night..." He winced with pain and shifted his leg to a more comfortable position. "I am not sure I could have made it to the ladder by myself. But her arm was strong around me. She is a most unusual young woman, Tiger. Now, if you will help me up I will stand watch while she is in the galley."

A most unusual young woman. Tiger ran a tired hand across his face. He thought that he loved her. At least he knew that he loved being with her and that he cared what happened to her. But he wished she was safely back in Hong Kong or in that town in Ohio she had come from. He was not sure who their pursuers were, he only knew they were dangerous and that he must protect Bethany from any harm.

An hour later Tiger found the group of islands he had been looking for. He guided the boat in among them, and when he found a place where he knew they couldn't be seen, he dropped anchor.

They would rest here for the day. When darkness fell they would press on for China.

Chapter 7

The air was so still that even the birds seemed suspended as they glided from tree to tree. The *Dragon* barely moved in the water. Just before dark, while Chang stood watch from a lounge chair on deck, Tiger and Bethany slipped over the side of the boat for a swim.

"Why is it so hot and still?" Bethany asked as she swam alongside Tiger. "The air feels almost too thick to breathe."

"It's possible that another storm is brewing but we're too far away to pick up any weather information."

Looking troubled, Bethany brushed the wet hair out of her eyes. "Couldn't we just stay here if there's a storm?"

Tiger looked at her as he trod water. He wanted to reassure her, to say that there would be no storm, that there were no men looking for them, that he would keep her safe from whatever danger lay ahead. And he would keep Bethany safe, he vowed. Once they were in Kwantung with his mother he would breathe more easily.

Tiger thought now of his mother. He had written before he left Hong Kong to say that he was coming but he hadn't told her he was bringing Ross Adams's daughter with him. Nor had he said that he was coming for the dragon.

Su Ching disapproved of the dragon business. The only arguments Tiger ever remembered occurring between his parents had been over it.

"Men have died to possess it," Su Ching protested each time his father brought up the subject. "It is an ancient object of great beauty that men have made into a thing of greed and violence."

"It's worth a fortune," his father always said. "A damned fortune! Ross and I risked our lives for the dragon; it belongs to us."

"No! It belongs to China!"

Tiger still remembered the look of his mother's face whenever she said those words. She had never been the docile Chinese wife of legend, and when she was angry hundreds of years of proud mandarin heritage and the blood of royal empresses showed in her face. Those were the times that his father—half in anger, half in jest—had called her the Dragon Lady. She was a formidable and indomitable woman, too much of a woman for his good-natured, easygoing father to handle.

His father had always backed down before Su Ching's wrath, and even now Tiger wasn't sure whether it had been because Bill Malone feared or loved his wife. But Tiger wasn't his father. His mother's blood ran in his veins, too. Almost from the time he learned to speak, Tiger had asserted himself. There had been endless battles while he was growing up, and if as he grew older, he sometimes let his mother have her way, it was because, like his father, he loved her.

In a few days Tiger would see her. He had never before introduced her to a woman and he had no idea how she would act. He had seen Bethany's bravery, but he didn't think she'd be any match for his mother. He had no idea what his mother's reaction would be when he told her that he and Bethany had come for the dragon.

Now as Tiger looked at Bethany he thought how soft, how vulnerable she was. He knew he should warn her about his mother, but he didn't want to harm whatever relationship might develop between the two women.

"You look tired," he said. "You should rest."

"I will later. I slept enough this morning." Bethany looked at him. "But you haven't had any sleep since we left the last port. You must be exhausted."

Tiger turned on his back and closed his eyes. "I am. Chang insists he's all right, so perhaps I will let him take the helm when we leave. Do you mind taking the first watch?"

"Of course not."

"I wish you didn't have to. I would much rather have you sleeping next to me."

Tiger flipped over and reached for her. Wrapping his legs around her body, he pulled her to him and kissed her, a long and lingering kiss. With his mouth still pressed to hers they drifted beneath the surface of the water.

Bethany's body was slick against his. He pushed the bikini top aside so that he could cover her breasts with his hands. The feel of the cool, erect peaks stirred him and he felt the urgency of passion warm his blood. Breathlessly they rose to the surface. Bethany clung to him for a moment, then quickly covered her breasts.

But Tiger wasn't ready to let her go. He kissed her again, more urgently this time, and pressed her close.

Bethany felt the hardness of him against the thin swath of cloth that covered her and knew that Tiger wanted her as much as she wanted him.

Breathlessly Bethany broke away. "Chang will see," she whispered. "You have to rest. You..." Her voice trembled. Tiger's eyes, as green as the sea, were warm with desire.

He urged her close again and covered her mouth with his. As they sank once again beneath the water his hand slid down her body, under the bikini bottom. His fingers were water-soft as they caressed her, inflaming her so her body was weak with desire by the time they surfaced. So weak with desire that she barely noticed that the sky had darkened until she felt the spatter of rain on her face and saw a flash of lightning split the sky as Tiger led her toward the boarding ladder.

"I'm going to rest," he told Chang when they were aboard. "Bethany will relieve you in a half hour."

Chang nodded. "I doubt they will find us here, Tiger. Nevertheless, it is wise to keep watch." He smiled at Bethany. "There is no hurry. Rest too if you wish."

"No, I..." Her legs trembled so much that she could hardly stand. "No, I'll be up in a few minutes. I just want to shower and change."

"If you want to shower," Tiger said when they were in the companionway, "then we will shower together." He opened the door of his cabin and when they were inside he quickly stripped off her suit, then his own, and led her to the shower.

A warm stream of water coursed down on them as Tiger took a bar of soap from ledge and began to lather his hands. Slowly he ran them down Bethany's shoulders to her breasts. Even more slowly he rubbed his hands over their rounded fullness, lingering on the erect nipples, gently tugging, flicking the soap away so that he could see the apricot buds.

"Wait." Bethany took the soap from him and lathering her own hands rubbed them across his chest and around his back. As she did so, Tiger turned so that the full spray of water hit her, rinsing the soap from her body. Then, as her soapy hands moved lower he began to kiss her breasts. She moved to cup his buttocks, running her hands over them before she slid around to touch his maleness. Frantically his tongue flicked against her breasts and his teeth closed on a ripened bud.

Her desire mounting, Bethany whispered, "Oh, darling."

The sound of her voice inflamed him. Quickly he dropped to his knees. Droplets of water clung like tiny pearls to her springy blondness as he parted her legs. Her hands curled in the midnight blackness of his wet-slick hair. She closed her eyes and felt the jet of water once more as Tiger's mouth, his sensual, demanding mouth consumed her. Almost too weak to stand Bethany clung to him, whispering his name over and over again, "Tiger, Tiger. Oh, please." And did not know what it was she pleaded for as wave after wave of pleasure flooded through her.

When her legs trembled and her body began to tighten, Tiger said, "Not yet, Bethany. Not yet, my love."

Bethany's body was on fire as she whispered his name in a frenzied litany of desire. She was lost, a prisoner of the hands that held her and of the mouth that so sweetly tortured.

Suddenly Tiger let her go. He came up beside her and together they stood under the cascading water. Then quickly he turned the water off, and not even taking the time to dry either of them, he picked her up and carried her to his bed.

Before she could speak he entered her. "Bethany!" His breath rasped against her throat. "Oh, Bethany."

Tiger's body was thunder and lightning against hers, as primitive and uncontrolled as the elements. For a moment Bethany was overwhelmed by his intensity, then her body responded. She was lost in him, a part of him as he carried her higher and higher on a sweeping tide of passion.

It was more than she could bear. Her body tightened just as Tiger cried out and covered Bethany's mouth with his in that final rending, glorious moment of fulfillment.

Lingering, pulsating, their two hearts beat as one as they slid slowly, sleepily, back to earth.

When Tiger finally slept, Bethany slipped away from him. She dressed quickly in a pair of white shorts and pulled a T-shirt over her head. Barefoot she stood by the bed, gazing down at him, filled with the love she felt for him, knowing nothing would ever be the same for her again. "I love you, Tiger Malone," she murmured, "I'll always love you."

Then she went up on deck to relieve Chang.

They left the protection of the islands that evening. Cautiously Chang maneuvered the *Dragon* out through the rain to the open sea. Bethany stood on the bridge, wearing Tiger's yellow slicker over her shorts, the binoculars to her eyes, scanning the horizon. There was a sail in the distance, headed east of them, but nothing else.

In spite of the rain the sea was calm. Bethany felt no fear now. It was as though all of her fear of the unknown, all of her uncertainty, had been washed away by the rain and by the realization of love, a love that had shaken her to the very depths of her being.

Bethany lifted her face to the rain, exultant in her love as she whispered his name once more. For more than an hour Bethany kept to her post. When her eyes grew tired she went to the wheelhouse. Chang's face looked strained. She knew that his leg pained him, but in spite of it, he had insisted on taking a turn at the helm. She went below to prepare a light meal, then had him show her how to take the wheel so that he could eat and rest for a few minutes.

"Do you think there'll be another storm?" she asked.

Chang shook his head. "Only rain." He took a sip of his coffee. "But it will slow us down. If it clears up we should reach the mainland early tomorrow morning." He took a sip of his coffee. "I will stay with the boat while you and Tiger travel to Tsingyun." He hesitated. "Have you ever met Madame Su Ching?"

Bethany shook her head. "Do you know her?"

"Last winter she came for a two-month visit to Hong Kong. She is a most...unusual woman, of French and Chinese heritage I believe. She is very beautiful and she is very strong. Poor Lee Tung was terrified of her."

Bethany looked at Chang curiously. "Why?"

"She is a formidable woman. She turned Lee's galley upside down and fixed it the way she wanted it. There is no doubt it is more efficient now, as is Lee, but Tiger had to give Lee a substantial raise to keep him from leaving."

Bethany took a sip of her coffee as she digested this bit of information. She hadn't given much thought to Tiger's mother, but now she felt a sense of unease; she knew that Tiger planned to leave her with his mother while he went in search of the dragon. Chang's words only strengthened Bethany's resolve not to be left behind in Kwantung.

The rain stopped a little before midnight. At twelve-thirty Tiger came out on deck.

"Why didn't you wake me?" he asked Bethany. "You must be exhausted."

"I'm a little tired but I can hold out for a few more hours. Chang needs to rest more than I do. I'll stand watch while you relieve him."

"No." Tiger looked up at the sky still covered with clouds. "We'll drop anchor and I'll stand watch. You and Chang go to bed."

Bethany moved closer to him. "Do you really have to stay up on deck? I'd sleep much better with you beside me."

"You wouldn't sleep at all, sea witch," he said with a low growl. "Now get below before I clap you in irons."

"Aye, aye, Captain," Bethany said as she saluted, and with a smile turned and went down to his cabin.

When Bethany awoke at daylight she heard the hard slash of rain against the portholes. She threw back the sheet, stepped out of bed, and found herself running sideways across the floor. She hung onto a bolted-down chair and tried to regain her balance. The room was too hot. Her stomach quivered. She lurched to the closet, grabbed her jeans, a shirt, and sneakers, quickly put them on and headed for the door.

The sea was gray; foam-topped waves spewed over the *Dragon*'s bow. Bethany took a deep breath and ordered her stomach to behave as she made her way to the wheelhouse. Tiger was at the helm, an almost fiendish look of pleasure on his face.

"A foul weather day," he said happily. Then he saw Bethany's face. "Are you all right?" he asked.

"I will be." She took a deep gulp of air.

"Perhaps if you eat something you'll—"

"Please." She held up her hand in protest. "Please don't talk about eating."

"Did you take one of those pills I gave you the first day?"

Bethany shook her head. "I don't think I could swallow water right now."

"You don't have to." Tiger reached behind him, opened a drawer and brought out a box of pills. "You can chew these," he said as he handed them to Bethany. "Take one and you'll feel better in a little while."

Tiger knew how terrible she felt. To take her mind off her stomach he pointed to his right and said, "You can see China, Bethany. We will reach land in an hour or two."

"Fine," she said between clenched teeth.

Tiger's dark brows came together. He wanted very much to take Bethany in his arms, but he knew that wouldn't help. Instead, in a firm voice, he said, "Chang has been on watch for almost three hours. I'd like you to relieve him."

"But I'm..." Bethany's shoulders straightened. She shot him an angry look and said, "Yes, of course. I'll go down at once."

Tiger handing her his slicker, said, "Put this on," then turned back to the wheel.

Bethany staggered down the ladder mumbling, "Aye, Aye, Captain Bligh," knowing how Mr. Christian had felt just before the mutiny. She zigzagged her way to the bow and when she reached Chang he fastened a safety line around her waist and said, "Rough day."

Bethany nodded as she gripped the rail.

"Are you all right?"

She took a deep breath and felt salt spray on her face. "Yes," she said, "I'm all right."

I'm all right, all right, all right, Bethany repeated to herself for the next fifteen minutes. And suddenly it was true, she *was* all right. She even felt a thrill of excitement. China loomed in the distance; this part of the journey was almost over. Today she would set foot on that ancient land, the land that was a part of Tiger's heritage. The search for the golden dragon had begun.

Chapter 8

It was a little before noon when the *Dragon* rounded the tip of Po On Peninsula. Tiger decreased his speed as he entered the bay and headed toward a cluster of wooden buildings. Immediately several uniformed men ran out onto the pier and signaled a docking space.

Carefully Tiger maneuvered the boat up to the dock. He turned off the engine, then hurried to help Chang throw out the mooring ropes.

The men in the blue uniforms were armed. Their expressions were serious and impassive as helpers grabbed the ropes and secured the boat. Tiger saluted the officers and spoke to them in Chinese.

"Tiger is identifying himself and requesting permission to go ashore," Chang told Bethany. "One or two of these men are with the port authority. The others are probably immigration and customs."

"But why do they look so grim?" Bethany asked in a low voice.

"It is the universal expression of all government officials," Chang said with a slight smile. But his smile faded as two of the uniformed men boarded the boat and barked a question to Tiger.

"They want to know what we are carrying," Chang whispered. "Next they will ask to see our papers. Are your passport and visa in order?"

Bethany nodded. She didn't know what she had expected her entrance into China to be like, but she'd assumed it would be like Hong Kong where everyone had been courteous, even affable. One of the officials said something to her and she turned nervously to Tiger.

"Show him your passport," he said.

Bethany held out her papers. The man took them, looked at the photographs, then at Bethany. He stamped the passport and put it in his pocket as he turned and started off the boat, nodding for them to follow.

"Where is he going with my passport?" Bethany asked nervously.

"To the immigration office." Tiger took her arm. "Don't worry. I've never come in here by boat before, but I am sure it's standard operating procedure."

S.O.P., Bethany thought. I certainly hope that's all it is. She looked around her at the dull brown buildings, the stark, dry landscape. Everything seemed so bleak and desolate, even the thunderclouds that hung low on the horizon as though waiting for a chance to growl.

Another uniformed man sat behind a battered desk. He eyed them suspiciously and took the three passports from his officer. "What is the purpose of your visit to China?" he asked.

"We have come to visit my mother," Tiger said. "Chang Lu works for me. Miss Adams is my fiancée."

"Why do you have an American passport?"

"My father was an American; my mother is Chinese."

"Will the three of you be traveling together?"

"No, Chang Lu will stay with the boat. Miss Adams and I will travel together to the home of my mother."

"In what city?"

"Tsingyun."

"Your mother's name?"

"Madame Su Ching. She is of the family of Ching Wu-Chien."

"Ching Wu-Chien?" The official's voice changed imperceptibly. "An old and honorable family." His fingers drummed against the three passports for a moment. Then he handed Tiger both his passport and Bethany's. "I will keep Chang Lu's passport until the two of you return," he said. "The train station is twenty kilometers from here. Tomorrow morning at eight I will have one of my men drive you there. It connects with the train for Canton. From there you can take another train to Tsingyun."

"Thank you," Tiger said. "That would be most kind." He hesitated. "Are we the only boat that has stopped here in the last few days?"

"Yes." The official's eyebrows rose in question. "Why do you ask?"

"There was a boat similar to ours that seemed headed this way. I was curious, that is all." Tiger picked up his and Bethany's passports. With a nod to the assembled officers he led her out of the building.

A guard followed them out and stayed four paces behind all the way to the boat. When they were aboard he took up a position facing them.

"At least you will have company when we're gone." Tiger smiled wryly at Chang.

"We must be thankful for all things," Chang said with a self-mocking bow.

"I'm sorry that you must stay here; I hope it won't be for long. What worries me the most is that the other boat might tie up here and give you trouble."

"I doubt they would stop at an official port. I think they will look for a secluded place and try to avoid immigration."

"Perhaps you're right." Tiger looked at Bethany and when he saw the worried look on her face he took her hand and said, "I hope the uniforms haven't alarmed you. I know this place is pretty bleak, but the scenery and everything else will be different when we leave."

Bethany glanced around her at the terrain, and finally at the dock where the man in the blue uniform, his rifle cradled in one arm, stood guard. She wanted to tell Tiger that it was all right, that she wasn't afraid. But she was; afraid of this place and of these strange men. Hong Kong had been so different. It was a civilized, cosmopolitan city where she had seen almost as many European and American faces as she had Chinese. But this wasn't Hong Kong, this was China. Bethany took a deep breath and summoned a smile.

With as much conviction as she could muster she said, "I suppose all borders are alike. I don't know what I expected . . . a welcoming committee and a red carpet, maybe. Grim looking types with rifles are not my idea of friendly."

Tiger relaxed. He knew Bethany was still afraid, and he understood how different this was from anything she'd ever known or experienced. All of it, Hong Kong, the storms at sea, their being pursued and shot at, was beyond the realm of anything she'd ever known. Even this relationship between the two of them must seem new and strange to her. She was on unfamiliar territory, about to embark on what could be a dangerous venture in an alien land.

Tiger would try to make the transition easy for her, but he knew that the days ahead would be difficult for both of them.

He put his arm around her. "It will be better tomorrow," he promised. "Once we are on our way to Canton things will look brighter."

The warmth of his embrace comforted her. Bethany closed her eyes and leaned against him. Yes, she thought, tomorrow everything will be all right. When we're away from here and on the train.

The train bulged with people. What seemed like hundreds more fought to board. Tiger gripped Bethany's arm to propel her through the crowd. "Most Chinese trains have a soft and a hard section," he said as he helped her aboard. "I hope this one does."

"Hard and soft?"

"That's like first and second class in the West." Tiger turned as a uniformed attendant tried to shove past them and spoke in rapid Chinese. The man shook his head and hurried on to the next car.

"Only one class." Tiger took Bethany's arm. "Come on, let's see if we can find a seat."

The seat was a wooden board, jammed together with other wooden boards. Tiger placed their two small suitcases under the seat as they squeezed into a space between an elderly woman who held a small child on her lap and a man with two live chickens at his feet. The small child, a round-faced boy with a bowl haircut, stared at Bethany with big black eyes.

More and more people crowded into the car, until they stood shoulder to shoulder and thigh to thigh, like sardines in an antiquated wooden box.

"We'll change trains in a few hours," Tiger said. "I'm sure the next train will be better than this."

Bethany nodded, too overwhelmed by the crowd of humanity surrounding her even to speak. It was hot; the only air—hot air—came from the open windows. The people around them were silent, staring at her with open curiosity as the train began to chug out of the station. She sat up straight, tucking her feet under the seat, then bent down to adjust the suitcase that Tiger had placed there.

As she did she glanced at the feet of the elderly woman seated next to her. The woman's feet, crippled by binding, were unbelievably tiny, no more than five inches in length. For one long moment Bethany stared, then quickly sat up. A feeling of sick horror overwhelmed her and she tried not to look at the woman.

All of this was alien to her. But this was China, Tiger's world. He wasn't wearing a Mao jacket like most of these people. He was taller and better dressed than they were, but he was one of them. She wasn't, and never would be.

With a feeling that was very close to tears, Bethany closed her eyes so that she would not see the curious stares.

They changed trains at a place called Chinghen. This time they were able to sit in the "soft" section, and for the first time since they had docked yesterday, Bethany was able to relax.

From Chinghen it took only three hours to reach Canton. "Guangzhou," Tiger told her. "Canton is the western name. The dialect here is almost incomprehensible to other Chinese but I speak it well enough to make myself understood." He saw the smudges of fatigue under her eyes. "It's a modern city, Bethany. You'll feel better after you've had a shower and something to eat."

"I know." Bethany brushed her damp hair back from her face and stared out of the open window at the approaching city. She saw factory smokestacks, Buddhist temples, television antennae, pagodas, wooden shacks, European-style homes, high-rise buildings, hotels. And bicycles, thousands and thousands of bicycles.

China, she thought. This is China.

The White Swan Hotel was on the shores of the Chu River. It boasted a multilevel atrium with waterfalls and gardens, an arcade of shops, and large, airy rooms.

"Why don't you shower?" Tiger said when he put their bags on the bed. "I'll check on the train to Tsingyun and try to send a telegram to Mother." He put a finger under Bethany's chin and smoothed her hair. "You look tired. Why don't you rest before dinner?"

Bethany looked at him for a long moment, then quietly leaned her head against his shoulder. I'm tired, she wanted to say. But I'm afraid, too, afraid of this strange and ancient land that is your heritage. Afraid to love you because of who you are.

But Bethany didn't voice her fears. She kissed him quietly and without passion and told him that she would bathe and rest and then she would be fine. After he left she took off her clothes. She showered and washed her hair and after toweling it dry she lay down on the big mahogany bed. She remembered the curious stares of the people on the train. From outside her window she could hear a chorus of bicycle bells.

The bells of Canton, she thought. Then she slept.

Bethany was still asleep when Tiger came in two hours later. He put a package on the bed, then sat down next to her. Her lips were slightly parted, her cheeks flushed. One hand curled against her cheek, the blond hair tumbled loose on the pillow. She looked very young and vulnerable and for a moment Tiger felt a wave of tenderness that rocked him like a physical blow. He put his hand on the curve of her hip and when she didn't respond he bent to kiss her temple.

"Wake up," he whispered against her skin. "It's time for dinner."

Bethany sighed. Without opening her eyes she reached up, encircling his neck, and brought his face to hers to kiss him, lazily, sleepily, murmuring his name against his lips.

"Bethany...?"

Silencing him with a kiss, she began to unbutton his shirt so that she could reach her hand inside and touch his skin. She heard the rasp of his breath as her fingers tangled in the thatch of his chest hair, then reached to fumble with his belt buckle.

Gone for the moment were her doubts and fears. She was lost in a dream, carried away on a tide of warmth and feeling and the sheer pleasure of awakening to his touch.

Tiger threw back the sheet. He found her breasts through the thin material of her nightgown. She whispered her pleasure and his mouth covered hers.

"Wait." Tiger moved away from her. Bethany opened her eyes and watched while he removed his clothes. Her lips, moist and inviting, were parted as the tip of her tongue darted out to touch the corner of her mouth. Her breath came in quickened gasps.

Tiger looked down at her. He felt the thud of his heart against his ribs, the almost painful swelling of desire. Slowly he pulled back the sheet. In a voice made harsh by need he asked her to sit up and when she did he pulled the gown over her head and tossed it aside. Then he was beside her, his mouth crushed against hers, feeling the silken loveliness of her against him. Her hands came up around his shoulders, caressing, urging him closer, and he knew that they couldn't wait. It had to be now. Now, quickly, urgently, or they would burst with wanting.

With a cry Tiger rolled Bethany beneath him. Hands on her hips he thrust himself into her, moaning aloud as her softness closed around him. His mouth covered hers. He caught her lower lip between his teeth, holding it tight while he ran his tongue over it. He bit the corners of her mouth, almost beside himself with need. Then, afraid of hurting her, he pulled back. But when he did Bethany cupped his head and threaded her fingers through his hair, to bring him again to her lips.

Her body lifted to his, demanding as he demanded, on fire with the need to have him closer and yet closer.

"Bethany...ah, Bethany..." Tiger's arms tightened around her as he rocked her close, all sense of reason lost in the pleasure of the moment.

Bethany's body rose to his. Her hands tightened on his shoulders. She was lost in the arms that held her, in the lips that kissed her, in the body that possessed her, and that she too possessed.

When she cried his name he breathed in the sweetly desperate words of her fulfillment as his own body exploded, carrying him higher and higher as, with fevered words, he told her how he loved her.

Later, after they had showered together, Tiger gave her the package that he'd placed on the bed. Inside was a cheongsam, a Chinese dress of rose-pink satin. Peacocks in vivid shades of blue were intricately embroidered onto the material.

"It's beautiful," Bethany said in a breathless voice.

"Wear it tonight."

The satin was smooth against her fingers. She looked at Tiger. "Thank you," she said. "Thank you, darling."

The dress fitted as though it had been made especially for her, molding her breasts and her hips, coming just below her knees. She fastened the buttons high on the mandarin collar, stepped into her high-heeled pumps, and turned around so that Tiger could look at her.

He took one step forward, but he didn't touch her. "You're one of the most beautiful women I've ever seen," he said in a hushed voice. Then he watched as she brushed the golden hair back from her face and fastened pearl drop earrings in her ears.

Again Tiger felt the beating of his heart against his ribs. But this time it beat without passion; it beat with an intensity of love that shook him to the very depths of his soul.

But he did not speak of his love as he took Bethany's arm and led her down the curved marble stairs to the dining room. There he ordered swallow's nest soup, vegetables in black bean sauce, chinjew chicken, and moon cakes for dessert. And all the while his mind returned to Bethany—his love.

Chapter 9

The home of Madame Su Ching was in the European section of Tsingyun. When the pedicab stopped in front of it Tiger said, "Usually a home this size is divided into several apartments, but because of my mother's old family connections she has been allowed to keep her home the way it is."

Bethany looked at the tree-lined street, so different from the other parts of the city that she and Tiger had just driven through. There had been small homes, tar paper shacks, Buddahs of every size, green-roofed temples and five-tiered pagodas. Hundreds of people had crowded the busy streets where bicycle bells drowned out every human sound. But here it was different. This street, this house, exuded a quiet, old-world elegance.

"Come, we'll go in," Tiger said. "I'm sure my mother is waiting."

Nervously Bethany smoothed the skirt of the tailored blue dress she'd worn for traveling. Chang's words about Tiger's mother being a formidable woman came back to her. If Madame Su Ching hadn't approved of poor Lee Tung, how would she feel about her son bringing a strange American woman to her home?

The door was opened by a servant woman. Scarcely five feet tall, the woman looked up at Tiger through eyes crinkled with age.

"Ni hau?" she said. "How are you, honorable sir?"

Tiger bowed. "I am well, Mai Ling," he said in Chinese. "This is Miss Bethany Adams. Is my mother at home?"

"She is waiting for you, sir." The old woman bowed as her eyes flicked over Bethany in curious appraisal.

The corridor Mai Ling led them into was clean, and cool, the beamed wooden floor polished to a high gleam. When she came to an ornately carved door she paused, then sliding the door open bowed and stood aside so they could enter.

Silk hangings decorated one wall. A five-panel screen, brilliantly designed in startling colors of red and gold, green and fuchsia, stood beside a cherry wood desk. Chinese chairs, carved with intertwining dragons, were placed around the room. Scarlet peonies in a lacquer bowl bloomed from an ebony table inlayed with mother-of-pearl. At the far end of the room, next to a stone fireplace, there was a red velvet sofa. As Bethany and Tiger crossed the floor a woman rose to greet them.

Su Ching's face seemed carved of pure, unblemished ivory. Her black hair was pulled back from her face into a chignon, and her dark eyes, fringed with long black lashes, framed by pencil-thin eyebrows, were almond shaped. She was quite tall and as slender as a girl. She wore a black cheongsam, black silk stockings and high-heeled black pumps. She was, Bethany thought, a strikingly handsome woman.

"Mother!" Tiger reached her in three long strides. He put his hands on her shoulders and kissed her cheek. "You're more beautiful than ever," he said in English as he held her away from him. "I have missed you."

"As I have missed you, Tiger." A pale hand caressed his face. "It has been much too long. I hope you have come for a long visit." Her glance slid to Bethany. "I see you have brought a friend." Her voice grew hushed. "How nice."

"Bethany." Tiger held out his hand, motioning her forward. "Mother, this is Bethany Adams. I'm sure you remember her father, Ross Adams, Father's friend."

A momentary frown marred the smooth forehead before Su Ching held out her hand. On one manicured finger there was the largest jade ring Bethany had ever seen. "Yes, of course I remember Ross," she said in a liltingly musical voice. "How do you do, Miss Adams. Did your father accompany you to China?"

"No, Madame Ching. My father died several months ago."

The delicate eyebrows rose. "Oh? I'm so sorry." She motioned to one of the carved chairs. "Please sit down."

Bethany sat quietly while Madame Ching talked to her son.

"I was surprised to receive your telegram," Su Ching said to Tiger. "I could not imagine whom you were bringing with you." Her gaze flicked to Bethany. "I hope you'll find the room I have prepared for you comfortable, Miss Adams."

"I'm sure I will. I hope I'm not putting you out."

"Of course not." Su Ching looked up as the door opened and Mai Ling entered, followed by a manservant carrying a silver tray. "I thought you might enjoy a cup of tea after your journey, Miss Adams." Before Bethany could answer Su Ching turned to Tiger. "You flew to Canton?" she asked.

"No, mother, we came by boat."

"By boat? But that must have taken days. Why in the world would you do that?"

"I hadn't ever taken The Dragon on a real cruise. This seemed like a good opportunity. We docked on the Po On Peninsula. Chang stayed with the boat."

"And Lee Tung?"

Tiger hesitated. "Lee remained behind on one of the islands we put in to."

"I see." Su Ching's face looked puzzled as she poured the green tea and handed a cup to Bethany. "How long can you stay in Tsingyun, Tiger?"

"I'm going to leave in a few days, Mother. But if it is all right with you, Bethany will stay here."

Again the eyebrows rose. Carefully Su Ching put her teacup back on the saucer. "Are you here on business then?"

"Yes, Mother, but perhaps we can discuss it later."

She appraised him with her black almond eyes and seemed about to speak. Then changing her mind she took another sip of her tea. When she had finished it she turned to Bethany, and ringing a small brass bell on the ebony table next to her chair said, "I'm sure you are tired, Miss Adams. I will have Mai Ling show you to your room."

Bethany looked at Tiger, then away. "Thank you," she said, knowing she'd been dismissed. "Yes, I am tired."

He stood up as Mai Ling came into the room. Taking Bethany's hand he said, "I will see you later."

"We dress for dinner, Miss Adams." Su Ching's voice was cool. "And we eat promptly at seven-thirty."

Bethany's lips tightened. Barely resisting the impulse to bow, she forced a smile to her lips, and with a brief nod followed the elderly servant out to the corridor.

They climbed a curving staircase. Silently they went down a long hall, past closed doors. When at last the old woman opened one of the doors, she motioned Bethany to enter, said something in Chinese, and bowed herself out.

A large bed dominated the room. It was covered by a heavy red and gold brocade spread that matched the draperies hanging from the floor to ceiling windows. There was a lacquer bedside table, a writing desk, a chair. At one end of the room there was a cherry wood armoire and when Bethany opened it she saw that her dresses had been hung and her other clothes and shoes neatly arranged on the shelves.

With a sigh she went to the windows and pulling back the curtains looked down on the courtyard below. It was a small yard, made lovely by blooming apricot trees and a circle of pink and red tulips. When Bethany opened the window the scent of apricot blossoms drifted up to her. Her hand tightened on the curtain. She didn't know what she'd expected Tiger's mother to be like, but she hadn't expected the cold and haughty woman who had greeted her. She wouldn't stay here; when Tiger left she would leave with him.

Resolutely Bethany turned away from the window. After she had undressed and bathed in the claw-footed tub in the adjoining bathroom, Bethany lay down to think. For a while, she'd been able to believe that she and Tiger were only a man and woman who had fallen in love with each other. Now, here in his mother's house, Bethany was reminded that they were from two disparate worlds. He was East, she was West. It was obvious that his mother would never accept her.

At seven o'clock Bethany rose and went to the armoire. She looked at the lovely cheongsam that Tiger had given her and knew that it would be more than acceptable. But with a frown she put it back in the closet. It seemed to her that it was necessary to make a statement. She was not Chinese, she was an American, and tonight she would look like an American.

At twenty-five after seven, dressed in a lemon-yellow sheath, and high-heeled sandals Bethany descended the stairway. She paused with her hand on the carved newel post, gazing through the open doors to her right into the dining room. From the glow of candelabra she saw that the room was empty. For a moment she hesitated, uncertain. Then from above Tiger said, "There you are. I didn't know where Mother had put you so I knocked at several doors." He quickly came down the stairs, dressed in dark trousers, a white silk shirt, and a brocade dinner jacket. His eyes took in the blond hair fluffed about her face, and taking her hand he brought it to his lips. "You're beautiful, Bethany."

Bethany touched his face. She started to speak, then stopped abruptly.

Madame Su Ching stood below looking up at them. Her floor-length cheongsam was Chinese red, and matching red butterfly sticks jutted from her chignon. Her face was impassive. Seconds ticked by before she spoke. "Shall we go in to dinner?"

At dinner Tiger sat on Su Ching's right, Bethany on her left. A white linen cloth covered the table that was set with fine china and chopsticks.

"Would you prefer a fork?" Su Ching inquired as Bethany fingered the sticks.

"No, thank you." Bethany had had very little experience with chopsticks, but she was determined to manage.

The meal began with dim sum, hors d'oeuvres. That was followed by shark's fin soup, for which a spoon was supplied, a vegetable dish of mushrooms, gingko nuts, spring onions and bean sprouts, and finally roast duck. The duck was the most difficult to manage, but when Tiger asked if she'd like a fork she politely declined a second time.

He smiled at her as he served spiced rice wine and tried to include her in what little conversation there was. When the dishes had been cleared and a bowl of fruit had been placed on the table, Su Ching asked

Bethany about her mother and when Bethany told her that her mother was ill and in a convalescent home, Su Ching said, in a disapproving voice, "I am surprised that you would leave her with strangers."

"I had no choice." Bethany took a sip of the wine. "My father made me promise that I would come to Hong Kong after he died. He wanted me to see Mr. Malone...your husband."

Su Ching regarded Bethany over the rim of her wineglass. "I find that odd," she said. "My husband and your father rarely corresponded. They hadn't seen each other for years."

"I know." Bethany looked across the table at Tiger. "He...my father asked me to bring a letter to your husband."

"It must have been a very important letter to make you leave your mother when she was ill." Su Ching's almond eyes were cold.

"Bethany's father wrote to Dad about the golden dragon," Tiger said. "He thought it was time to go and get it."

Two bright spots of color appeared in the ivory cheeks. "And you, my son, do you think the time has come to get it?"

"Yes, Mother, I do."

Su Ching looked at Bethany, then at Tiger. "So this...this woman has persuaded you to come to China for the golden dragon." Her voice was angry as she faced Bethany. "Can you not leave things alone? The golden dragon has been hidden for forty years. Why must you disturb it now? Don't you know how dangerous it might be for my son to attempt to take it out of China? Men have killed each other over it for hundreds of years? If anyone knew that the two of you had come to China to find it—"

"There are people who already know," Tiger said.

"What do you mean?"

"Bethany and I were attacked on the Star Ferry dock a few nights after she arrived. At first I thought the two men were only after her purse, but when we discovered her room had been ransacked I knew it had to be more than that." His voice hardened imperceptibly. "And let me make it clear, Mother, Bethany didn't persuade me to come to China. It was my decision."

"Was it?" Su Ching's gaze shifted to Bethany. "Tiger has been content to leave the golden dragon where it is. If you had not come he—"

"Mother!" Tiger put a restraining hand on her arm. "That's enough! You know that father wanted me to have the dragon some day. He would have taken it himself if you hadn't stopped him. It's time to take it out of its hiding place."

"No!" Madame Ching rose from her chair. "The dragon belongs to China, not to some avaricious American. I will not permit it. I will not—"

"That's enough!" Tiger's voice was sharp as Bethany pushed back her chair and ran from the room. She started toward the stairs, then saw Mai Ling, her wrinkled face startled, blocking the staircase just in front of her. Without conscious thought Bethany ran past the stairs, down a corridor, and seeing a door opening into the darkness plunged through it. Then she smelled the scent of apricot blossoms and knew that she was in the courtyard.

She ran to one of the trees and leaned against it, her hands covering her eyes. She'd been a fool to come here with Tiger, a fool to think that his mother would accept her. She didn't need the golden dragon, she didn't want it. She'd go home. She'd sell the house so that she could take care of her mother. She—

A sudden noise came from behind her. Bethany turned and looked up just as a figure dropped from the old stone wall to the ground. Before Bethany could move a second figure appeared at the top of the wall. She opened her mouth to scream but the scream froze in her throat as the first man sprinted forward. Before she could cry out he grabbed her shoulders. Dear God! It was the same man! The man on the dock in Hong Kong! The man who had grabbed her ankle the night that Chang was wounded!

Bethany screamed, and the sound, shrill and clear cut through the night air. A hand clamped over her mouth. Hard hands held her. The other man dashed forward and together the two men forced her toward the wall. Bethany fought against them but knew even as she did that they were too strong for her. Frantic with fear, she bit the hand that covered her mouth and when he let her go she screamed again.

A light flashed on, illuminating the courtyard.

"Bethany!" Tiger cried.

Struggling, she turned her head and saw him in the doorway, his mother a step behind him.

But Tiger was too late, he couldn't save her now. The two men had her almost to the wall. One vaulted to the top of it. Flat on his stomach, he shouted down to the other man and held out his hands to receive her. Bethany cried out, rammed her elbows back, and with a surge of strength broke free just as Tiger ran across the courtyard toward her. She heard his mother's voice calling him back. She saw the man who had held her pull a gun from his belt.

As though in slow motion he raised the gun and pointed it at Tiger—a perfect target, framed in the light from the open door.

A cry tore from Bethany's throat as she flung herself at her captor. She felt his breath against her face, saw his eyes, small and black as death so close to hers. She heard a sharp ping, then a blaze of fire seemed to rip through her side. She fell back a few steps as her vision began to cloud. From somewhere she heard Tiger calling her name and tried to tell him it was all right, that everything was all right. But then the darkness closed in around her.

A cool hand touched her forehead. A voice said, "You are safe now. The doctor is on his way. Please don't be afraid."

"Tiger!" Bethany struggled up out of the depths of the night that surrounded her. Her eyelids fluttered open. "The man with the gun . . ."

"Tiger is safe. He is bringing the doctor."

Bethany tried to sit up but a white-hot pain seared her body and she fell back. She opened her eyes again and looked up into Madame Su Ching's almond-shaped eyes. Su Ching took her hand and spoke to her again, gently, soothingly. Bethany tried to speak but the pain and the blackness took hold of her again and she drifted into unconsciousness.

The next time she awoke Tiger was beside her. "Bethany?" he said. "Bethany, can you hear me?"

She tried to speak, but the words didn't come. Her face was pale, her lips white and bloodless. The doctor had told him that the bullet that pierced her side had only cut through her flesh. Her flesh! Tiger had wanted to throttle the doctor. He wanted to take Bethany's pain and make it his own. As long as he lived he would never forget the sound of her scream, the sight of her being dragged toward the wall. He'd seen the gun as he ran forward but his only thought had been to rescue Bethany, to get to her before she reached the wall.

He heard his mother scream. He saw Bethany's face, white with fear. Then she'd flung herself on her captor. She'd taken the bullet that had been meant for him.

By the time Tiger reached her the two men had fled over the wall. It didn't matter—they didn't matter. Bethany lay crumpled on the grass beneath the apricot trees. He'd gathered her in his arms as his mother ran to his side.

"My God," Su Ching said in a breathless voice, "she threw herself in front of the gun."

Tiger had given his mother one swift look of anger before he picked Bethany up and ran into the house. "Stay with her," he had barked after placing her gently on a couch, and ran down the street to the house of Dr. Feng Yen-Chi and had all but dragged the aging doctor back to his mother's.

Dr. Feng had cleaned and bandaged the wound. "Give her these pills when she wakes," he said. "Then one every four hours. I will return in the morning."

"Bethany?" Tiger said again as he smoothed the fair hair back from her face. "Bethany?"

She opened her eyes. "What time is it?" she asked.

"Almost midnight. How do you feel?"

"Strange." She licked her lips. "May I have a drink of water?"

"Of course." Tiger held the glass to her lips. She drank, then lay back against the pillow. "I'm not sure I remember what happened." Her voice was weak. "Did someone hit me?"

"No, Bethany, you were shot."

"Shot?"

Tiger could see the confusion on her face, then the remembering as she reached out and touched his hand. "You're all right," she said. "They didn't...I thought they were going to shoot you. The gun...the gun was pointed at you. I thought...I thought..." Tears trickled down her cheeks.

Tiger looked at her. He knew now that he loved her more than he had ever thought it possible to love. He wanted to tell her but couldn't speak because he was choked with love. Instead he gently kissed the tears from her cheeks and held her close.

Bethany sighed against him as her hands cupped his face, his dear face. "Tiger," she whispered against his skin. "Oh, Tiger."

A soft knock on the door made her release him. Bethany leaned back against the pillow as Madame Su Ching entered. Tiger's mother looked at her, then to Tiger she said, "I have prepared a medicinal tea for Bethany. Would you bring the tray up, please?"

"Of course, Mother." He squeezed Bethany's hand. "I'll be right back," he said.

When he went out of the room Su Ching approached Bethany's bed. "I am glad to see you are awake. How do you feel?"

"As though I've been run over by a rickshaw."

A slight smile crossed Su Ching's face. Then her face sobered and she stepped closer to the bed and dropping to her knees she took Bethany's hand in hers. "I ask you to forgive me for my unkindness," she said in a low voice. "I thought you were an interloper and that you were trying to take my son from me." She lowered her head. "But you have given me my son, not taken him away and for that I can never repay you. I can only thank you."

"Madame..." Bethany's voice was tentative. "Madame, please. It's all right, I understand."

"And you forgive?"

"Of course I forgive."

And Tiger, standing at the door, saw the two women he loved most in the world smile at each other.

Chapter 10

A week passed before Bethany was allowed out of bed. Even though her wound was not serious there was the danger of infection, and Dr. Feng came every day to bathe the wound, change the dressing, and administer an evil-smelling tea.

The police had been notified immediately after the attack, but no trace had been found of either man. On Tiger's insistence a guard had been posted at Madame Su Ching's house.

Once the pain of the wound passed, Bethany was able to enjoy her recuperation. She rested a great deal and when she wasn't resting either Tiger or his mother was with her. Su Ching had changed since the evening of the attack. Though still reserved, her attitude toward Bethany had warmed. She prepared meals especially for her—baked fish, chicken broth enriched with noodles, and soups of every variety.

Su Ching didn't speak about the golden dragon. Instead she told Bethany stories about Tiger, what he had been like as a boy, and brought out a photo album so Bethany could see for herself what a handsome child he had been.

"He has his father's green eyes," Su Ching said. "That is the only part of Bill that Tiger has—the eyes and that ridiculous name Bill insisted on giving him."

"It rather fits him though, doesn't it?" Bethany smiled.

> "Tyger! Tyger! burning bright
> In the forests of the night,
> What immortal hand or eye
> Could frame thy fearful symmetry?"

"William Blake," Su Ching said with a nod. "Yes, that does rather describe him, doesn't it? Especially on the night you were wounded." She took a deep, shaking breath. "I've never seen my son look like that. I don't like to think what might have happened if you...if the wound had been more serious." Su Ching covered her eyes with her delicately shaped hands. "He would never have forgiven me, Bethany. Nor would I have forgiven myself. I sent you running out into the courtyard. I—"

"No, please, Madame, it wasn't your fault. I'm all right now. Or I will be if Dr. Feng and Tiger ever let me out of bed. Tiger barely lets me move; he watches over me all the time."

Even at night Bethany would awaken to find Tiger sitting beside her bed. If she stirred he immediately moved to comfort her. On the second night, when the pain had been bad, he had lain beside her, murmuring to her until the pain receded and she fell asleep again. She had never known such tenderness. She'd been an unusually healthy child, and her mother had rarely needed to soothe her this way.

Her mother. That was one of the things Bethany fretted about. The day after the shooting she told Tiger of her concern.

"No one knows where to reach me if Mother needs me," Bethany said. "What if she gets worse? What if she needs money for something?"

Tiger had told her he'd take care of it. That day he had gone to the telegraph office and sent a message and money to the nursing home, giving them his mother's address in Tsingyun. He thanked God that things were better between his mother and Bethany. If his mother's attitude had not changed he would have had to send Bethany back to Hong Kong when he left to search for the dragon. But his mother *had* changed; now he could leave Bethany, knowing that she was safe and that she and his mother got along. As soon as Bethany was well he would leave.

Tiger had tried to broach the subject with his mother one afternoon when Bethany was sleeping. "You know where the dragon is, don't you?" he had asked.

Su Ching had given him what his father had sometimes called her Dragon Lady look.

"It's time, Mother," he said. "My father and Bethany's father knew that if they did not go after the dragon that some day their children would."

"You don't need the money," Su Ching said coldly.

"No, but Bethany does. I want it for her."

"The dragon belongs to China."

"It belongs to whoever has it in his possession. For forty years it belonged to Father and to Ross Adams."

Su Ching's face remained completely still. "Was not what happened the other night warning enough? Those men tried to kidnap Bethany, and if they had succeeded they would have tortured her until she told them where the Dragon was, or they were convinced she didn't know. Then they would have killed her." She dug her red-lacquered nails into Tiger's arm. "Do you want this so much that you would risk her life?"

"Of course not. The men who came here the other night will be more careful now, as I will be. When I leave, Bethany will stay here with you."

"I will not let you risk your life."

"I am a man; I will do what I think is best."

On and on the argument went. Nothing was settled. Su Ching still refused to divulge where the golden statue was hidden.

The first night that Dr. Feng permitted Bethany to come downstairs, dinner was a festive occasion. Scarlet poppies contrasted with the fine white tablecloth. Bone china and silver gleamed in the reflection of candlelight. Su Ching presided over the table, stately and elegant in a royal-blue cheongsam that almost matched Tiger's dinner jacket. Bethany wore the pale-green satin dressing gown and matching brocade slippers that Su Ching had brought to her room that afternoon.

"Something new will make you feel better," Su Ching had said. "I ordered it the day before yesterday. I had to guess your size. I hope you like it."

Bethany ran her fingertips over the smooth green satin. "It's beautiful," she said. "Thank you, Madame—"

"Su Ching. Please call me Su Ching, or Su if you prefer."

Bethany smiled shyly. "Su Ching," she said.

Later, when Bethany dressed, she looked at herself in the mirror. She had lost weight this past week; her eyes seemed enormous, against her pale, thin face. With a sigh she brushed her freshly washed hair letting it cascade in soft waves to her shoulders. Then the brush stopped and a slight frown drew her eyebrows together. She had changed. It wasn't just the gown or her thinness, it was more than that. It was as though the young woman from Tiffin, Ohio, had somehow faded into the background and been replaced by a different person. Someone who had been touched by life and by love. Tiger had changed her, and she would never again be the woman she had been before.

Now Tiger looked across the table at her. Her skin looked iridescent, her gray eyes luminous in the glow of the candlelight. He felt his heart expand with the need to touch her. Unable to help himself, he rose from his chair and came around to her side of the table to put his hands on her shoulders and brush his lips against her golden hair. Then he tilted her chin up, saying, "I haven't thanked you properly for what you did, Bethany. It should have been me who received that bullet, not you. I owe you my life."

Bethany couldn't speak. She could only gaze into his eyes, feeling as though her very bones were melting. Everything was forgotten at that moment; it seemed to her that she looked into the very heart of Tiger Malone.

"There is an old Chinese saying," Su Ching said softly, "that whoever saves a life is responsible for that life forever."

Bethany looked at Su Ching and saw the concern, the warning in her eyes.

"Tigers do not tame easily, Bethany."

Bethany held her breath. With the slightest of smiles she said, "But a tiger is such a magnificent beast. Why would anyone want to tame him?"

Now it was Su Ching's turn to smile. "Why, indeed?"

Tiger looked from his mother to Bethany, not at all sure he liked this exchange. He was about to speak when Su Ching said, "Will you pour the wine, dear?"

And the moment passed.

The dinner was delicious, the conversation light. Bethany felt stronger than she had since the attack, but by the time the spiced pears were served her strength had begun to ebb.

"You're tired," Tiger said. "Let me take you to your room."

"Just another sip of wine." Bethany smiled at him. "It's such a relief to be out of bed."

"I know," Su Ching said, "but Tiger is right. This is your first night downstairs, you must not overtax yourself."

Tiger pushed his chair back, but before he could speak Mai Ling entered. She spoke rapidly to Su Ching, then handed her an envelope. Su Ching's pencil-thin brows came together. "It is a telegram for you," she said as she handed the envelope to Bethany.

Bethany's mouth went dry as she stood up and took the envelope.

"Would you like me to read it to you?" Tiger said.

"No...no, I'll read it. It must be from the nursing home. Perhaps they were alarmed when they received the cable saying that I was in China. They're probably still worried about the money for Mother." But even as Bethany said the words she knew that wasn't what the telegram was about. She began to tremble, and handing the telegram to Tiger, whispered, "Yes, please read it."

He opened the envelope. As he took out the telegram Su Ching stepped closer to Bethany. He read and his shoulders tensed. He looked at Bethany. "I'm sorry," he said. "I'm so very sorry. It's your mother."

Bethany closed her eyes.

"She died in her sleep a week ago. The person who sent it from the nursing home says they are waiting for your instructions." He put his arm around her. "Will you let me take care of it?"

"Yes." Bethany's voice was only a whisper.

"Let me take you to your room now."

She was frozen, unable to speak or to move until Su Ching touched her face. She looked at her and saw the shared pain, the compassion in the dark almond eyes. Then Su Ching's arms were around her, holding her as she wept for the mother she had lost, for a door that had been closed forever.

When at last the crying stopped Su Ching released her to Tiger. He swept Bethany up in his arms and with his mother beside him, carried her up to her room. The tears began anew when he put her on the bed.

Su Ching sat down beside her and smoothing the fair hair back from Bethany's pale face, said, "Tiger will stay with you tonight." She kissed Bethany's brow, and with a look at her son went out and closed the door.

For a long time Tiger held Bethany and when at last she stopped crying he undressed her. Then he removed his clothes and got into bed with her. He pulled her close so that her head rested in the hollow of his shoulder. Without words Tiger offered her a transfusion of his love, and held her until at last she slept.

Bethany was quiet in the days that followed. At times she spoke to Su Ching of her mother. At other times she sat in the courtyard under the apricot trees without speaking. It seemed to her now that all of the ties to her past had been broken. She knew that never again would she return to the life she had known before, for now there was no one there to return to. She felt adrift, a leaf torn from a branch, floating alone on the wind, looking for a haven.

"Bethany?"

She looked up then into Tiger's green eyes. She wondered if he was her answer; if she could live the kind of life he would expect her to live if they committed themselves to each other.

Tiger had never spoken of commitment. In the days that had passed since her mother's death he had been kind and gentle. He had shared her bed, comforted her when she cried out in the night, and soothed her tears. They hadn't made love, and Bethany knew he was waiting until the first terrible grief began to ebb.

He spoke her name again and this time she answered, "It's all right, Tiger." She covered his hand with hers. "It's time we looked for the dragon."

"We?" He shook his head. "No, Bethany, I will look for the dragon. You'll stay here with Mother so that I know you're safe."

The gray eyes grew dark as Bethany shook her head. "I'm going with you." Her voice was firm. "Part of the dragon belongs to me. If I'm to share in the riches then I must also share in the danger."

"No! You will do as I say. You will—"

"I have brought some tea," Su Ching said from the doorway. She paused, looking from one angry face to the other, then with a sigh came out into the courtyard. She put the tea tray down on the table and when she had poured it and taken a seat she said, "You were arguing when I came out. Was it about the golden dragon?"

Bethany glanced at Tiger, then away, waiting for him to speak.

"Yes, Mother. Bethany wants to go with me when I look for it. I have told her that is impossible, that she is to stay here with you until I return."

Su Ching's face was impassive.

Tiger put his teacup back on the saucer. "It's time, Mother, time for you to tell me where to find it."

Su Ching sipped her tea as she looked from her son to Bethany. "I will tell you," she said. "But first I will tell you a story."

"Mother!" Tiger's voice held an edge of impatience. "We want to hear about the dragon."

"And you shall." Su Ching took a deep breath and began: "The Sung Dynasty ruled China from the year nine hundred until 1279, when the empire extended from the Great Wall to Hainan. It has been said that the golden dragon dates back to the year one thousand.''

The almond eyes closed. ''But long before, in the beginning of the beginning, there lived in a small village on the island of Hainan a maiden so pure and so beautiful that all who passed her way were stuck by her beauty and her goodness.

''Her mother named her Flowering Peach, for even at birth her skin was that fruit's softly shaded color. Her father, a rich merchant involved in trade with Persia, had little interest in his girl child. But as Flowering Peach grew into womanhood he began to think how he might use her to gain more riches for himself.

''Like all females of her age and time, Flowering Peach spent her days helping her mother with the household chores and tending her garden. One day, in the spring of her sixteenth year, a young poet passed through the village. He saw the girl in her father's courtyard and before she could move away he began to play to her on his lute. In song he told her that her skin was as delicate as rice paper, her hair as fragrant as jasmine.

''The next day the poet appeared again, and again for many days thereafter. He was a handsome young man. His body was as slender and as strong as a sapling, his eyes as dark as the midnight sky. Each day the poet and Flowering Peach fell more and more in love.

''Then one day a rich merchant from Persia came to the village to buy silk from the girl's father. She was sent for. 'Bring tea,' her father ordered, all the while looking slyly at the expression on the fat merchant's face.

"Flowering Peach brought the tea and after she had served it and left the room the merchant said, 'I would have your daughter.'

"'What will you give me in return?' her father asked.

"'One thousand gold coins.'

"'It is done,' was her father's reply.

"The next day he told Flowering Peach that he had sold her to the merchant from Persia. The merchant, he said, had other business in China, and would return for her in two weeks' time. She prostrated herself before her father. Weeping, she told him of her love for the young poet and begged to be allowed to marry him. But her father would not listen to her pleas.

"That night Flowering Peach told her lover that they must part. Together they wept and he said to her, 'Come away with me. We will defy your father; we will marry.'

"Fearfully Flowering Peach looked at him. She was afraid, but her love was greater than her fear, and that night the lovers slipped away together into the darkness.

"Her father found them a week later and brought them back to the village. His daughter had been despoiled; the despoiler must be punished. In a rage the father sought a sorcerer. He paid him one hundred silver coins to cast a spell upon the poet, an irreversible spell that turned the handsome young poet into a hideous dragon with ugly green scales and distended fire-breathing nostrils.

"Flowering Peach looked in horror at the dragon, but instead of backing away, almost blinded by her tears, she tenderly ran her fingers over the ugliness of scales. And with her touch of love the dragon turned into an object of golden beauty.

"But love could do no more than that; the poet had been locked within the golden dragon for all eternity.

"Her father had won. He convinced the Persian merchant to buy Flowering Peach although she had been soiled.

"The night before the wedding Flowering Peach slipped from her father's house. In one hand she held a flacon of a deadly potion, in the other the golden dragon. Down through the willows she went, down to the river. There on the moss-green banks, by the light of the moon, she drank the poison. With her last breath she held the golden dragon to her breast and whispered of her love.

"And as she died one single tear fell from the dragon's eye."

There was silence in the courtyard as Su Ching finished her story. She sat back in her chair, relaxed, eyes closed, as the last rays of the afternoon sun faded from the horizon. When at last she spoke she said, "The golden dragon is a symbol of a love that will never die. Its value cannot be measured by money."

Impatiently Tiger got up from his chair. "It's only a story," he said. "A legend that has nothing to do with reality."

"Doesn't it?" Su Ching turned her gaze to Bethany. "Do you think it is only a story?"

"I . . . I don't know. It's beautiful and sad. I don't know," she said again.

"Nor do I." Su Ching looked at her son. "Now I will tell you where you can find the golden dragon," she said.

Chapter 11

As the shadows of evening descended on the courtyard, Madame Su Ching drew her chair closer. "Your father met Ross Adams in the early part of 1939," she said to Tiger. "Chennault had been hired by Chiang Kai-shek to train Chinese pilots in the fight against the Japanese, and other pilots, adventurers from Italy, England, France, and America, came to China to fly with Chennault. They became the Flying Tigers, brave and daring men who, with one hundred and fifty Chinese pilots, flew planes no sensible man would have taken two feet off the ground."

"Did you know your husband then?" Bethany asked.

Su Ching shook her head. "No, I didn't meet Bill Malone until later when Chennault moved his base of operations to Kunming. It was the summer of 1941. I had just turned seventeen." She smiled at Bethany. "I will never forget that summer. Kunming is called the City of Perpetual Spring because all through the year there is a profusion of blossoms: cherry, camellia, magnolia, azalea and plum. To me it is the most beautiful city in China.''

For a moment Su Ching was silent, remembering. Then she said, ''I met Bill and Ross one Sunday afternoon in the park. My father had taken all of us, my sisters and brothers and me, boating on the lake.'' Her lips curved in a smile. ''They were so young, so raucous and full of life. So glad to be alive.

''They waved to my sisters and me and though we smiled behind our fans we dared not wave back. Then, Bethany, your father stood up in the boat and began signaling to us, doing funny things to make us laugh. Suddenly, before we could warn him that this type of Chinese boat had not been built for such antics, the boat overturned.''

''Father went overboard?'' Tiger asked with a grin.

''And came up with a lily pad covering his face. He looked so funny that my father took mercy on both of them. We helped them rescue their boat and get back to shore, and father invited them for tea.

''My father—your grandfather, Tiger—admired the pilots who flew for Chennault. He thought they were brave and wonderful men, but he did not like the idea of his daughters becoming friendly with foreigners because of the cultural differences, the barriers that are almost impossible to cross.'' Su Ching looked at Bethany. ''But there are times,'' she said, ''when two people look at each other and there is a magic, a destiny that cannot be denied. Then nothing matters except that these two people should be together. That is the way it was with Bill Malone and me. Not even my father could stop the love we felt for each other.''

In the silence of the garden a mourning dove called to its mate. Bethany looked at Su Ching through the gathering darkness. She knows, Bethany thought, she knows what I feel for Tiger.

"Bill and I were married by a Catholic missionary in Guilin," Su Ching went on. "Ross Adams was our witness. No one in my family was there." She closed her eyes and after a moment said. "For our honeymoon trip we hired a small boat and went down the Li River to Yangshuo. I still remember the feathery bamboos lining the banks, the cormorant fishermen, the local people who sold tropical fruits. And the way Bill Malone looked with the sun on his face."

Su Ching lowered her head for a moment. When she spoke again her voice held a different tone. "I didn't learn that Bill and Ross were dealing in the black market until a year after we were married. I was angry when I found out, and I tried to tell Bill how dangerous it was. He laughed and said, 'Dangerous? What in the hell could be more dangerous than what I've been doing for the last couple of years? The planes we're flying are put together with spit and glue. We land on runways that aren't fit for jackrabbits. Hell, girl, all the pilots are doing black market business. It's the only way we can put some money aside for when the war's over. *If* it's ever over. All we're doing is a little trading—cigarettes and liquor, silk, porcelain and jade. Things like that.' ''

Su Ching turned to Tiger. "I kept my peace until the day your father bought me this ring." She rubbed the fingers of her other hand across the large jade ring. "I knew it was expensive, that we couldn't afford it, and when I pressed him he told me about the golden dragon."

Her voice dropped to a whisper so that both Bethany and Tiger had to lean forward to hear. "He and Ross had been away for almost a month, on a mission to The Great Bend of the Yellow River. It was there, in that region where the capitals of eleven Chinese dynasties have flourished, that your fathers were given the golden dragon by a warlord who knew his enemies were closing in around him. He paid Ross and Bill a great sum to take the statue to his son who lived in northern China in a city called Jiayuguan.

"The fighting was fierce in those days, and many months passed before they were able to make the trip to Jiayuguan. They did, however, on one of their missions, return again to the Bend of the Yellow River. They went to see the warlord to tell him they had not yet been able to deliver the dragon. But when they arrived they were told by the few of his men who were still alive that most of their men had been killed, and that the lord himself had been tortured and murdered."

Bethany's hands tightened in her lap and she shivered, not sure whether from the evening chill or fear. She looked at Tiger and saw that he too was affected by his mother's story.

"Both Ross and your father were sobered by the news, Tiger. But I honestly do not think they connected the murder to the dragon. Not until they flew to Jiayuguan, and found that the son of the warlord's fate had been the same."

With trembling hands Su Ching smoothed her flawless hair. "They kept the statue in our home, wrapped in silk in a wooden box. For a long time I didn't open the box, but one day, while Bill was away, I took the box from its hiding place and slowly unwrapped it." She looked from Tiger to Bethany. "I have never seen anything as beautiful, as magnificent as the golden dragon. I touched it and it seemed so real that I could almost feel it quiver beneath my fingers."

Su Ching pressed her hands to her face and for a long moment did not speak. Then in a faltering voice she said, "I had heard the legend of the golden dragon when I was a child. I knew of its cultural value and I...I felt, after I had seen its beauty, that it should be in a place where all could see. I asked Bill to turn it over to the Chinese government.

"He refused. He said that it was ours. Then he and Ross took it to a place where they knew it would be safe. 'When the war is over,' he said, 'we will get it.' But when the war was over your father and I had to flee to Hong Kong. And China closed its doors behind us."

"Where is the dragon now, Mother?" Tiger asked.

"It is near Wuhan." And to Bethany she said, "Wuhan is a port stop for the Yangtze River steamers. It is a composite name for three cities, Hankow, Hanyang, and Chungtai." Her voice dropped to a whisper. "The dragon is in the monastery in Chungtai." She took a key from her pocket and handed it to Tiger. "Here is the key that with Bethany's key will unlock the place where the golden dragon is hidden."

Then quietly, not waiting for Bethany or Tiger to speak, Su Ching got up and went into the house.

Bethany sat as though frozen, her heart thudding hard against her ribs. In a voice made tense by emotion she turned to Tiger and said, "When do we leave for Chungtai?"

"Not we," Tiger said half an hour later as they were getting ready for bed. "You're not going anywhere."

"But—"

"I will not even discuss it, Bethany. I will go to Chungtai alone. When I have found the dragon I'll return for you. Together we will go back to Hong Kong where we will find a dealer and dispose of the dragon."

"Dispose of it?" Bethany looked at him incredulously, "How can you say that? The golden dragon isn't a . . . a *thing*. It's a symbol of love. It represents love!"

"Surely you don't believe the story my mother told us. She said herself that it was a legend, Bethany, a fairy tale she heard when she was a child." Tiger smiled at her stormy face and putting his hands on her shoulders he turned her to face him. "It was only a story, Bethany. There never was a girl named Flowering Peach or a handsome young poet who was turned into a dragon by an angry father." He gave her a little shake. "You came to China to find the dragon, Bethany. Well, we have almost found it, don't back out now."

"I won't. It's just . . ." She buried her face against his chest. "I don't know. I have a funny feeling about it. I wonder now if we should go after him."

"After *him*?"

"The dragon."

Tiger smiled at her. "My funny girl," he said softly. "My very dear and very funny girl."

They had not made love since they had been in his mother's house, at first because Bethany had been wounded. Later, although Tiger had slept with her, he'd known she was grieving over the loss of her mother. Now suddenly, all of the passion he'd held in check these last two weeks rushed to the surface. He wanted her so much his teeth ached, but trying to control himself he said, "We'll talk about this tomorrow. Now we will go to bed."

Bethany looked up at him. She saw the flame in his green eyes and felt the tension of his hands on her shoulders. "Yes," she said, "now we will go to bed."

With careful fingers Tiger unbuttoned her white silk blouse. He cupped her face. He kissed her eyes closed, kissed the tip of her nose and the sweet indentation that led to her lips. He took her lips softly at first, then with a cry his mouth crushed hers. He was hungry for her, dying for the taste of her, the feel of her. He slid down the straps from the wisp of lace that covered her breasts so he could cup them in his hands.

"Bethany," he whispered against her lips. "Bethany, I hunger for you."

Her knees grew weak. She clung to him as he swept her off the floor and placed her on the bed. Quickly he finished undressing her. Even more quickly he undressed himself, throbbing with desire. When she turned to snap off the light he said, "No, I want to look at you, Bethany. I want to see your face when we make love."

Gently, holding himself back, he kissed her. Tenderly he ran his hands down her body, stopping when he came to the still-red scar on her side, a memento of that awful night in the courtyard.

"I don't want to hurt you," Tiger said as he kissed the scar. "You must tell me if I do."

"You won't hurt me." Bethany put her hands on his shoulders to urge him on.

Tiger shook his head. Though he ached with the need to be inside her, he wanted to go slowly, to make passion linger and wait.

"Tiger..." Bethany's eyes were deep pools of silver gray.

He kissed her to silence, then trailed a line of fire down to her ears, her throat, and finally to her small, peaked breasts. With a sigh he turned Bethany toward him so that he could suckle first one, then the other. With each whispered cry he felt her body stretch with desire as she strained close to him. He left her breasts and with hot moist kisses, moved slowly down her body.

He kissed the inside of her thighs and heard her whisper his name. He stroked her and she quivered with passion.

Bethany couldn't bear it. Her body was on fire with longing. Oh, the sweetness of his mouth, the touch of his hands caressing her thighs. It was too much; it wasn't enough.

Suddenly, hands on his shoulders, Bethany pulled away from Tiger. She heard his startled gasp as she forced him under her, grasped his hips, then settled onto him.

Oh, the feel of him, the glorious feel of him inside her. He reached to caress her breasts and Bethany whispered her pleasure. She tried to go slowly so that this would last, but it was so wonderful. Her body ground against his and when his fingers tightened on the excited buds of her breasts she cried aloud, lost in frenzied pleasure as she strained toward that final moment of climax.

Through eyes almost blinded by passion, Tiger looked up at Bethany. Her eyes were closed, her face was wildly beautiful. Her body glowed with a fine sheen of sweat. He threaded his fingers through the golden mane of her hair and pulled her down to him. And it was too much. She cried his name and collapsed against him. He found her mouth, mingling his own cry of fulfillment with hers.

For a long time Tiger stroked her back. The soft cloud of her hair lay like silken threads against his shoulders and he turned to breathe in the scent of it. And of her. Bethany, he thought, will I ever get enough of your sweetness and your fire?

Long after she slept he held her and when, in the night, his passion began to grow again he rolled her beneath himself and slowly moved against her.

"I love you," Bethany whispered sleepily against his lips. "I love what you do to me." Her arms crept up around his neck and as she pressed her face close to his he felt her tears on his cheek.

"Darling," Tiger whispered. "What is it? Am I hurting you?"

"No, Tiger, no." Bethany pressed him closer. She wanted to tell him that sometimes she loved him so much, so far beyond words, that it frightened her. If he went away, if he left her... But because she couldn't tell him with words, she tried to tell him with her body. She lifted herself to him, yielding, giving all that she had to give until, shuddering in ecstasy, Tiger cried her name and surged with her in wonder and in joy.

Bethany held him against her breast while he slept. Tenderly she kissed his forehead and felt her body swell with love. She thought again of how Tiger had looked that night in the courtyard when her assailant leveled his gun at him. The moment was frozen in her mind. She heard again the click of the safety latch, saw Tiger, vulnerable and exposed. If she hadn't thrown herself at her captor, if she hadn't deflected the bullet...

Bethany closed her eyes and held him tight.

The next morning Tiger prepared to leave Tsing-yun. Bethany watched him pack, exhausted from the argument that had been going on since they had awakened. No matter how she had pleaded to go with him, Tiger's answer had been the same—an adamant *no*.

"I'll do whatever you say," Bethany said, determined to try one more time. "I'll stay behind in a hotel when we reach Chungtai. I—"

Tiger turned on her, his hand raised to halt anything else she wanted to say. "I will not discuss this again. You are to stay here with Mother until I return. Do not leave the house. Do not go out into the courtyard unless the guard accompanies you."

"Then I'm a prisoner?" Bethany was as angry as he was now.

"Yes, until I return." He came to her, and tilting her chin said, "I must know that you are safe, Bethany. That night, when you were shot, it was as though the bullet pierced my flesh too. I couldn't bear it if anything happened to you. I must know that you'll be here, waiting, when I return."

Her lips softened under his. When his arms went around her back to draw her closer, she allowed herself to sway toward him. He kissed her, hard, then let her go and began putting things into his suitcase.

Bethany watched him for a moment, then turned, and closing the door behind her, went downstairs. She found Su Ching in the living room, sitting at her desk.

"Tiger will leave this morning?" Su Ching asked.

Bethany nodded. "I want to go with him."

"And he will not let you?"

"No."

Su Ching replaced the plumed pen in the inkstand as she turned to face Bethany. In a gentle voice she said, "You are in love with Tiger, aren't you?"

"Yes, Su Ching."

"And he loves you." It was a statement, not a question. Red-manicured nails drummed impatiently on the desktop. "You are as determined as he to get the dragon and take it back to Hong Kong, to sell it to the highest bidder?"

Bethany nodded. "It belonged to my father, and to Tiger's father. It—"

"It belongs to China."

"But they risked their lives for it—and for China. Now it belongs to us, and to you."

"I want no part of it," Su Ching said angrily.

Bethany looked at Tiger's mother. "But your husband risked his life for it. He—"

"He died because of it!" Su Ching cried.

"What...what do you mean?" Involuntarily Bethany backed away.

"They killed him!" Su Ching's voice was filled with despair.

"Tiger didn't tell me. He didn't—"

"He doesn't know." Su Ching's hands, as delicate as an ivory fan, fluttered against her sides.

"Su Ching...?"

"They said it was an accident. They said that the car that came from nowhere, up over the curb onto the walk, was out of control. But that was a lie. I know it was a lie."

Bethany's breath caught in her throat. She wanted to say, how do you know? How can you be sure?

Su Ching, as though reading her thoughts, said, "My husband did not die immediately. When the police brought him to me he was still alive. He tried to tell me what had happened. The words were so faint I could barely hear him. His head was in my lap, so I put my ear to his lips.

"'It was them,' he whispered.

"Who, darling? I cried in my anguish.

"'Same men. Week ago after me. Recognized driver.' He clutched my hand. 'The golden dragon,' he said. 'They want the dragon.' Those were his last words," she said.

Cold, deadly fear gripped Bethany as she stared at Tiger's mother. For a moment she couldn't speak. When she could she said, "I need your help, Su Ching.

I want to go with Tiger but he won't let me. Please, I must go with him.''

For a long time Su Ching only looked at her. Then she nodded. "Yes," she said. "I will help you."

Chapter 12

"Bethany is upset," Su Ching said when Tiger was ready to leave. "She asked me to say goodbye to you."

"I'm sorry she's upset, but I want her here where I know she'll be safe." He saw the questioning look on his mother's face and added, "She'll be safe after I'm gone."

"Because whoever is after the golden dragon will follow you? Because you expect danger?"

Tiger rested his traveling case on the floor. "No, Mother, I don't expect it but I'll be prepared for it. If there's trouble I don't want to have to worry about Bethany. Besides, it will be easier for me to travel alone. I'm Chinese. I'm a man and I—"

"Ah, you are a man, therefore it is all right for you to go and for her to stay behind. Have we returned to the old days then? The days before the revolution?" The almond eyes flashed with anger.

The Dragon Lady, Tiger thought, half angry, half amused. He knew from experience that when his mother was in this kind of a mood no one could reason with her. Certainly his father hadn't been able to. He still remembered the hot flush of frustration rushing to his father's face when he was helpless against Su Ching's cold anger. "There's been many a time," his father had once told him, "when I'd like to take your mother across my knee and whale some of that Chinese stubbornness out of her." Then his father had grinned. "But somehow I couldn't see myself doing that to a princess of a royal dynasty."

Forcing himself to speak reasonably, Tiger took his mother's hands. "I can travel faster alone. Certainly I will be less conspicuous alone than I would be with an American woman. Bethany is young, she's... fragile. She wouldn't be able to keep up if there was danger."

"I thought she did rather well two weeks ago in the courtyard."

Tiger's lips tightened. "I will not argue about this," he said as he released Su Ching's hands. "I have to leave. I'll send a telegram to Chang Lu, then I'll catch the one-thirty train. Please say goodbye to Bethany for me. I know she's angry, but it'll be all right when I return with the dragon." He kissed his mother's cheek. "Take care of her," he said. "And of yourself." Then, before Su Ching could respond, he picked up his traveling case and quickly left the house.

Su Ching stood where she was. When the outer door shut she flinched, then closed her eyes in silent prayer. She hoped she had done the right thing.

* * *

The woman who boarded at the rear of the train was dressed in dark-green trousers, a Mao jacket and black slippers. Her hair was tied back by a scarf and covered with a wide coolie hat that partially hid her face. She sat in the back of the soft class car, head bent, an open book of Chinese poetry on her lap. When a worker pushed a cart with green tea down the aisle the woman accepted a cup without speaking.

The day was hot. Even the air coming in through the open windows seemed too warm to breathe. Other passengers stirred restlessly but the woman did not change her position.

The train passed through fertile river valleys, across broad plains where rice fields flourished, then began a slow ascent into the mountains. Slowing to a crawl, it labored painfully up the steep grades. When it stopped to take on a few passengers waiting beside the track, several people already on the train went to stand on the steps. One of them was Tiger Malone. He passed the woman in the Mao jacket without even seeing her.

When the train stopped at Xiamen, near the mouth of the River Jiulong, more people boarded. But all of them went to hard class. The woman ate a few rice cakes and drank from a bottle of mineral water.

Thirty minutes out of the port city of Fuzhou the train wheezed to a stop. Passengers shifted in their seats and looked out of the windows. A conductor scurried up and down the aisle, speaking in rapid Chinese. Twenty minutes went by. The train didn't move. The passengers grew restless and one by one they left their seats to wander out to the door.

Tiger stood up and stretched, then he followed the others down the aisle. There was only one person left in the car now, the woman with the coolie hat.

"It's very warm in here," Tiger said pleasantly in Chinese. "It may be some time before we leave. Wouldn't you be more comfortable outside where it is cooler?"

The woman didn't respond. Her head was bent so that he couldn't see her face.

"Are you ill? Perhaps I could get you some tea."

Still there was no response.

"Madame?" Tiger looked at her curiously. She was so still it seemed she didn't even breathe. There was something... something about the slope of her shoulders, the feet so precisely together... His muscles tightened. With a growl of anger he lifted the brim of the coolie hat and found himself looking into clear gray eyes, slightly tilted by makeup, and a face that had been darkened by one shade.

"Hi," Bethany said, trying to smile. "It's hot, isn't it? Maybe we should go stand outside."

Tiger stared at her, then without thinking, so angry he wanted to shake her, he yanked Bethany to her feet. "Damn it," he roared, "what in the hell are you doing here?"

"It was a nice day for a train ride and I—"

Her coolie hat fell forward, covering her face as he grasped her shoulders.

"Let me go!" Bethany tried to struggle out of his grasp, unable to see, and unable to get away from him.

"I told you I wanted you to stay with my mother. How dare you disobey me?"

Bethany broke away from him. She raised her hat so that she could look at him, as angry as he was now. "Disobey?" Her voice rose. "*Disobey*? Who do you think you are? Some feudal lord ordering his subjects around? I'll do what I want to do and go where I want to go. And I'm going to Chungtai."

"Not with me you aren't."

Her lips tightened. "Then I'll go alone."

"No you won't," Tiger bit out. "When we get into Fuzhou you will take a train back to Tsingyun. My mother must be frantic with worry. She—" His expression darkened. "I'll be damned, she knew you were going, didn't she? She helped you!" He rubbed one finger against her cheek, and his finger smudged the dark makeup. "The makeup, the clothes, she arranged for everything, didn't she?"

"Because she knew I was right, that I should go with you." Bethany lifted her chin defiantly. "I've come this far, Tiger, I'm not going to retreat now. You send me back to Tsingyun on one train and I'll catch the next one going to Chungtai." She put her hand on his arm. "Please," she said, "I don't want to fight about this—about anything. I want to be with you, I want to know for myself that you're all right. I couldn't stand not knowing if you were safe."

Tiger looked down at her. His face was harsh, the green eyes still narrowed with anger.

"Please," Bethany said again. "Please, darling."

"If I let you come you will do exactly as I say? Without argument?"

"I promise." A wave of relief flooded through her. It was easy to say that if he didn't take her she would make her own way to Chungtai, but the idea of making the trip alone scared her senseless. Maybe that was all that really did scare her, the idea of not being with Tiger. With him she knew she could face whatever danger might lay ahead. She trusted him and she believed in him. He would take care of her; she would take care of him. He was still angry, but she could handle his anger. What she couldn't handle was being left behind.

They left the car but before they did, Tiger said, "When we return take the seat you had. It would look strange if you came to sit with me or I with you." He looked down at her, his face still severe. "In China a woman would not behave as you have behaved. She would obey her husband without question or argument."

For one long moment Bethany glared at Tiger, then she tipped her head so that the coolie hat hid her face, hoping to look like any other Chinese wife being chastised by her husband. "Will we go on to Chungtai tonight?" she asked meekly.

Tiger shook his head. "No, the distance is too great. Depending on the schedule of the trains, it will take us three or four days to reach Chungtai. Tonight we will stay in Fuzhou."

And tonight I will soothe your anger away, Bethany thought. Tonight in Fuzhou.

The city, on the north bank of the Min River, was set in the midst of beautiful hills. Bethany, head lowered, followed Tiger away from the train station. The streets along the river weren't paved. All along the bank she saw people bathing in the same water where chickens were being plucked and washed, and chamber pots were being emptied. She paused for a moment, staring in fascination, then quickly hurried to catch up with Tiger.

When they reached the main section of the city the streets were paved and filled with bicycles. Tiger slowed his steps and looked around for a hotel. "Fuzhou was a port of call for Marco Polo," he told Bethany. "In the thirteenth century it was already a thriving commercial center for trade. It's not a city for tourists so the accommodations won't be what you're accustomed to."

"I didn't expect to stay in luxury hotels on this trip," Bethany said.

Without answering Tiger turned and walked quickly through a small park toward a group of buildings. One, a three-story gray building proved to be a hotel. When Bethany caught up with him, Tiger said, "Stay behind me. Keep your head lowered and do not speak." He strode into the hotel, with Bethany a few steps behind him.

When he had arranged for the room, paying the yuan in advance, he motioned with a jerk of his head for Bethany to follow him up the three flights of stairs.

In spite of her resolve not to utter one word of complaint, Bethany gasped when she entered the room. The bed in the corner was made of slats of wood covered with a straw-filled mattress. There were hooks for clothes on the wall, one chair, and a window without a screen.

"Well," Bethany said, trying to sound hearty, "this isn't so bad, is it?" She crossed the floor to the bathroom. Inside there was a toilet without a seat, a sink, one towel, and a rusted pipe jutting out of the wall for the shower. Quickly she backed out, not looking at Tiger.

The temperature in the room was stifling. She opened the top button of the Mao jacket and went to sit on the lumpy bed.

"Are you hungry?" Tiger asked.

"A little."

"Do you want to wash up before dinner?"

"No, just my hands. I don't want to wash the color off my face."

Tiger glared at her. "How did you persuade my mother to help you?"

"I'm not sure. I said I wanted to go with you and she understood how I felt; she thought that I should be with you."

"Damn!" He exploded with a string of Chinese words that made Bethany want to shrink back against the wall. Maybe I should have let him do this alone, she thought. Maybe I should have stayed behind. But no, Bethany knew even as she looked around the shabby room that this was where she belonged. Until they found the golden dragon, until this was over, she would stay by Tiger's side.

They found a restaurant around the corner from the hotel. Tiger ordered and when the dishes came Bethany saw that there was something that looked like fried fish, along with a vegetable dish. With it Tiger ordered beer.

"What kind of fish is this?" Bethany asked when she had eaten most of it.

"Fried eel."

Chopsticks poised midway between her plate and mouth, Bethany hesitated. "Oh," she said, then took the piece of fish in her mouth and washed it down with a long swallow of beer.

The room had cooled a bit by the time they returned to the hotel. Because there was no shade on the window they undressed in the darkness. Bethany took a short cotton nightgown out of her bag. "I'm going to have a shower," she said. And with an attempt at humor added, "I'll try to use only half of the towel."

When Tiger made no reply she went into the bathroom and closed the door.

The one thin stream of water was cold. Bethany washed with the almost unlatherable soap, scrubbed herself as well as she could, and waited forever for the stream of water to rinse her body. Out of the shower she dried herself and put on the cotton nightgown When she came out of the room, Tiger went in.

The straw mattress was lumpy, but more comfortable than Bethany would have thought. She pulled the sheet over her and moved back to the wall so that there would be room for Tiger. She felt strangely awkward and suddenly shy. Tiger was angry and she wasn't at all sure how she should handle his anger. She lay very still when the bathroom door opened and he crossed to the bed. He stood looking down at her for a moment, then without a word lay down beside her.

Bethany lay on her side, facing him. Tentatively she reached her hand out and touched his hip. He didn't move.

"Tiger?"

"Yes?"

"Are you sleepy?"

"No."

She took her hand away, but when she did Tiger's hand closed on her wrist and he brought it back and placed it on his hip. Slowly, hardly daring to breathe, Bethany began to stroke his thigh. He didn't move. Her hand went to his stomach. Her fingers caressed, stroking delicately up to his chest, curling in the patch of hair, lingering to circle a nipple before they began their downward travel to the flatness of his stomach.

Tiger didn't move or respond. Bethany touched his navel and began to follow the line of hair that led downward. She heard his indrawn breath, hesitated, then continued her descent. She touched him and he groaned, but didn't speak as she continued to caress him. Suddenly Tiger pushed her hand away. Without a word he rose up over her and pulled her into his arms. The heat of his skin burned through the thin material of her gown as he grasped her chin and held her while his mouth ravaged hers. There was no tenderness in him now, only passion and hunger. He bit the corners of her lips, taking her lower lip between his teeth to suckle and bite before he plunged his tongue into her mouth to engage her in a silken duel.

Breathlessly Bethany tried to break away from the arms that held her, but Tiger pushed her back against the straw. By the faint light in the room she saw his green eyes, tiger's eyes.

"Darling..." she began, but he stopped her words with a desperate kiss.

He pulled her gown over her head, he tossed it aside and his body covered hers, then his lips, warmed by passion, traveled to her ear. He bit the lobe and when Bethany cried out he soothed it with his tongue, circling to the curved inner part of her ear until she moaned with desire. The moan inflamed him and he moved quickly to capture a peaked blossom of her breast, and took it between his teeth, tugging and lapping and teasing until Bethany cried out again and tried to break free. When she did Tiger grasped both her wrists. He held them above her head and gazed down at her through eyes narrowed by passion. His mouth found hers again, ground against it so that she could feel his teeth against her lips before her lips parted to receive his tongue.

He took her breasts again, took them until she cried out, "No more! Tiger please . . . no more!" But when she tried to squirm from his grasp, he forced her closer to his hungry mouth.

Bethany had never known such anguished ecstasy. She couldn't bear it. Her body was on fire, begging for release. Incoherent sounds came from her lips to beg him to stop. But even as she begged she thrust her breasts upward to the mouth that so sweetly consumed them.

Suddenly Tiger released her. Frantically he parted her legs and thrust himself into her. With passion and anger he moved against her, holding her, covering her, possessing her as thrust followed angry thrust.

Bethany could no longer distinguish between the real and the unreal. A mixture of fear and desire overwhelmed her as she lifted her body to Tiger's. Her arms encircled his neck, her fingers dug into the flesh of his shoulders. With a groan his mouth found hers, demanding the response she willingly gave. His hands went around her back to raise her body to his as he plunged deeper and ever deeper into her feminine softness.

Whispers of frenzied joy burst from Bethany's lips as she clung to Tiger. This was the reality, this basic truth of male and female joined together in a passion as old as time. "Tiger—"

Again he silenced her with a kiss. It was too much, too long past bearing, as her body shattered into a thousand tiny pieces of luminescent fire.

Tiger's hands tightened, his body erupted in a frenzy of excitement that carried her further and further, again and again, up and up, until spent, she drifted down into his arms.

Tiger held her close to him, so close that she could feel the terrible thud of his heart against her ribs. His face rested against her throat, half covered by the cloud of her fair hair.

He kissed her shoulder and his breath was warm against her skin. "Will I ever get enough of you?" he asked in a hoarse voice. "Will I ever have all I want of your softness and your passion?" He raised himself and looked into her gray eyes. "There are times when I don't understand you," he said. "Times, like today, when I want to try to make you behave like a proper Chinese woman. Then I look at you, at who you are, and I know that I love you as you are. That I will always love you. Bethany, my fair Bethany."

For a long time after that neither of them spoke. At last Tiger began to move away from her, but when he did, Bethany said, "No, Tiger, stay." She kissed the top of his head. "Stay," she repeated, and held him until he slept.

Chapter 13

When Tiger awoke the next morning he stretched to ease the muscles that ached from lying too long in one position on the straw mattress. Then he looked at Bethany, curled up beside him. Her cheeks were rosy, her lips still swollen from the kisses of the night before. He tucked a strand of hair behind her ear and gently kissed her cheek. "Did you sleep well?" he asked.

"Mmm." She snuggled closer. "What time is it?"

"Almost eight."

"What time does the train leave?"

"There is no train to where we're going. I will have to arrange other transportation. It will be a long, uncomfortable trip, Bethany, because I want to travel by a circuitous route in case anyone is trying to follow us." He drew her closer. "In this moment I'm happy that you're beside me, but I wish you hadn't come."

"I wish you weren't angry."

"I'm not now, but I was yesterday. I was so furious when I saw you on the train in that ridiculous hat that I wanted to throttle you." He pulled back the sheet that half covered her. "I was still furious with you last night, and at myself for wanting to make love to you." He kissed her temple and in a low voice asked, "I was too rough, Bethany. Did I hurt you last night?"

"No." She felt hot color creep to her cheeks and tried to cover herself. But not before Tiger saw a faint bruise on the delicate skin of her wrist.

"I did hurt you," he said. "Can you forgive me?"

"It wasn't your fault, Tiger. I don't blame you for being angry. But please, don't be sorry that I came. I promise you that I'll do whatever you say. I won't argue when you tell me to do something and I won't complain. Just don't . . . please don't send me back."

"I have known very few American women," Tiger said musingly. "Mostly I have known Chinese or European women. You are different. You are so feminine one moment, so strongly determined the next. It's hard for me to understand you, to know how to behave with you."

"I thought men were intrigued by a little mystery," Bethany said with a smile.

Tiger looked down at her, half annoyed, half amused. "I am intrigued by you." He kissed her. "By these lips that are swollen from my kisses. By these breasts that quiver at my touch. As I am intrigued by your softness and your bravery and by the fact that I only need look at you and I want you."

Bethany came to him then, willingly, meltingly, lifting her body eagerly to his when he entered her, matching the rhythm of his movements with sharp little cries of pleasure. She clung to him when together they reached the summit and told him how much she loved him.

For that time together they were able to forget the danger that lay ahead of them.

Later, after they had washed and dressed, Tiger spread a map out on the bed. "We want to go to Nanjing," he said. "From there we will take a boat up the Yangtze River to Chungtai."

"Isn't there a train going to Nanjing?"

Tiger shook his head. "No, from here we will go to Wenzhou, then Chinhai by single track railroad. From there we will find transport to Hangzhou and on to Nanjing and Chungtai."

"It sounds arduous." Bethany paused, holding the sponge with which she'd been applying dark makeup to her face. "And interesting."

"It very well may be." Tiger watched as she put the sponge down and began doing her eyes. With a slight smile he said, "Your friends back in Tiffin, Ohio, should see you now."

Tiffin, Ohio. Bethany paused as she looked at herself in the mirror. It would be hot in Tiffin now. The corn would be tall... "Knee-high by the Fourth of July," her grandfather used to say. The beefsteak tomatoes would be red-ripe and better than any tomato in the world. Plums that her mother had used for plum dumplings would hang heavy on the tree in the backyard. But there'd be nobody to pick the plums this year, nobody ever again to make plum dumplings. Or potato salad and fried chicken for Sunday picnics at the lake, or... Bethany looked away from the image in the mirror and tried to hold back the tears that welled in her eyes.

"What is it?" Tiger asked, coming swiftly to her side.

"I...I was thinking about my mother. About home. It seems so far away this morning."

He rested his hands on her shoulders as he looked around the ugly room. "This must all seem strange to you." He leaned down and put his face close to hers and looking at their double image in the mirror said, "*I* must seem strange to you. We are very different, Bethany. The tint on your face, the pencil marks that seem to slant your eyes do not change who you are. You are West, I am East. Nothing we do will change that."

"Tiger..."

He shook his head, then straightened. "Let's have breakfast now, then I'll go to see about transportation." He watched as Bethany pulled her fair hair back off her face and bound it with a scarf. Next she would put on the Chinese clothes his mother had given her, then the coolie hat. But neither the clothes nor the hat would change who Bethany was—a woman from a world where he did not belong.

After they had breakfasted on sweet steamed buns and green tea, Tiger took Bethany back to the room. "I will return as soon as I can," he told her. "Don't leave the room and don't allow anyone to enter."

"I won't." She raised her face for his kiss.

When Tiger left he said, "Lock the door," and waited until she had. Bethany leaned against the door for a moment, then went to stand by the window and look down at the street. She watched Tiger leave the hotel and cross to the small park where several people were doing t'ai chi exercises. Tiger was dressed in a plain dark suit and well-worn shoes, but even so, there was something about him, his height, the way he carried himself, that set him apart from the other men on the street. Bethany smiled to herself as she watched him, but suddenly her smile froze. A man who had been doing t'ai chi turned to watch Tiger, then quickly slipped away from the others to follow him.

A child darted in front of Tiger. Tiger paused. The man behind him waited, lighted a cigarette, hesitating until Tiger resumed his walk.

Hands clenched tightly to her sides, heart thudding against her ribs, Bethany watched. Her first inclination was to run out and warn Tiger even though he'd told her to stay in the room with the door locked. But dear God, how could she run through the park without drawing attention to herself and to him? She looked at the man following Tiger. Her pulse quickened and she gasped aloud because she was sure, even at this distance, that it was the same man who had assaulted her on the dock in Hong Kong. He must have been following them—she had to warn Tiger.

Without a moment's hesitation Bethany ran out of the room and down the three flights of stairs to the street. Frantically she looked around and when she saw a pedicab she signaled to it, waiting impatiently while the man pedaled over to her. He said something in Chinese and Bethany suddenly remembered that she spoke not a word of that language. She grasped her throat, pointed to her mouth and shook her head. Then she pointed to the street at the far end of the park where she had seen Tiger and the man pursuing him disappear.

With a shrug the driver began to pedal. Bethany tapped his shoulder and with her hands in a revolving motion, indicated that she wanted him to go faster. When he shook his head she held up twenty yuan. The man grunted, then bent his back into his work.

Around the park they went toward the street at the far end. There was no sign of Tiger or of the man who followed him as the cab turned into the street. Where were they? Bethany thought frantically as the pedicab continued through an intersection. Then suddenly, ahead of her she saw the man who was following Tiger. The pedicab drew close to him, passed him. Bethany lowered her head so that the coolie hat covered her face. The street curved. At the end of it she saw Tiger. His pace wasn't hurried. He walked as though out for a morning stroll. When the pedicab drew abreast of him Bethany tapped the driver on the shoulder and motioned for him to slow down.

Tiger glanced up, away, then swung his startled gaze back to Bethany.

"Get in," she whispered. "There's a man following you."

Tiger's face tightened with anger but he got into the cab. "Damn it," he said under his breath. "I told you to stay in the room."

"But he was following you, the same man, the man from the dock, from Tsingyun."

"I bloody well knew he was following me," Tiger exploded. "I purposely led him down here so that I could confront him." His eyes were sea-green fury. "A few hours ago you promised me you'd do what what I told you to do."

"But—"

"No buts! You've disobeyed me again. And the worst of it is that now he knows you're traveling with me."

Bethany looked behind her. The man who had been following Tiger broke into a run. "Can't we go any faster?" she asked nervously as the pedicab turned a corner onto an unpaved street.

Not bothering to answer, Tiger tapped the driver's shoulder and thrust some money into his hands. The pedicab stopped. Tiger jumped from the cab. "Come on," he barked to Bethany as he grabbed her and sprinted down the street.

She followed, not daring to look over her shoulder, her mouth dry with fear. Tiger turned into a narrow passageway, drew her in and shoved her behind him. A moment passed. Suddenly he shot his hand out. He grabbed his pursuer by the throat, pulled him into the passageway, and slammed him against the brick wall. With a flick of the wrist the other man pulled a knife, but before he could thrust it forward Tiger yanked his wrist hard. A hiss of pain whistled through the man's teeth and the knife clattered to the street.

Tiger's arm pinioned the man's throat. "Why have you followed us?" he asked in Chinese. "Why did you try to take the woman in Tsingyun?"

"I tell you nothing!" the man gasped.

The pressure on his throat increased. Suddenly Tiger punched hard into the man's midsection.

Bethany flattened herself against the wall, hand to her mouth to keep from crying out.

Tiger struck again, the edge of his hand chopping his opponent between shoulder and neck. The man sagged but Tiger held him upright. "Who is behind this?" he demanded. "Who sent you after us?"

"He will kill me if I tell."

"I'll kill you if you don't." Tiger's hands went around the man's throat. "Tell me!"

"I cannot."

Tigers hands tightened. "In another five seconds you will die," he threatened.

The man's eyes bulged. "Weng..." he gasped as he tried to break free from the steellike fingers. "Please, you are killing me."

"I know," Tiger said flatly, relentlessly.

"Weng Tsan Tsi," the man whispered.

"Why?"

"Tiger," Bethany implored, "you'll kill him."

Ignoring her, Tiger held the man tight against the wall. "Why?" he growled.

"The dragon." The man's breathing was labored as Tiger loosened his grip. "He has waited for years for your father to make his move. Now it is you, you and the woman who pursue the statue. He has killed for it in the past." His eyes rolled upward. "He will kill me now."

"Why does he want the woman?"

The frightened eyes shifted to Bethany. "If he has her he knows you will tell him where the dragon is hidden."

"I should kill you," Tiger said. "But I will let you live so that you can take a message back to Weng Tsan Tsi. Tell him I'm not afraid of him. Tell him if he sends another man after me that I will kill that man.

If he ever again attempts to take the woman I'll go after him and kill him if it's the last thing I do on this earth." Tiger thrust the man away from him. "Tell him!" he said in a low and deadly voice.

Still shaken from what had happened, Bethany pressed her back against the rough wooden slats of the open truck and tried not to look at Tiger. She wasn't sure how he had arranged for them to ride in the back of the truck amid the piled sacks of grain. After what had happened in the passageway she had followed him wordlessly, not even objecting when, back at the hotel, he rummaged through both suitcases, threw out what he thought they didn't need, and crammed the rest into one case.

"Keep your head down," he'd ordered when they left the hotel. "Stay two paces behind me and do not speak unless I tell you to." His voice had been coolly impersonal and for the first time since she'd known him Bethany was afraid. This was a man she hadn't known existed, a street fighter, a man who, given the provocation, could kill. She was shocked, unable to equate him with the man she had fallen in love with.

It was late afternoon. The air was hot and still, the dirt road bumpy and filled with dust. Bethany wished she could unbutton the Mao jacket and take off the coolie hat. But knowing she couldn't, she closed her eyes and tried not to think about the heat. They hadn't eaten since the sweet buns and the green tea at breakfast. She was hungry but knew better than to speak of it. Tiger hadn't wanted her to come; now she wished with all her heart she hadn't.

At sunset they rattled through a village. "Kuaot'ou," the driver said.

"This is as far as he's going." Tiger took the bag, then Bethany's hand and helped her out of the truck. After he had paid the driver and watched him drive off to the left, he said, "We'd better try to find a place to stay."

Where? Bethany wondered as she looked around her. This was only a village of small, mean houses. She saw no hotel as she followed Tiger down the dusty street of the town.

"There's the market." Tiger started toward it. "I'll buy food for tonight and tomorrow."

Bethany followed him in silence, her head lowered so that no one could see her face, while he bought oranges and pears at one stand, then moved on to other stands. Past swimming eels, live frogs hooked together on a string and dead snakes, to buy buns, lotus nuts and roasted chestnuts. He handed all the bags to her and murmured, "It will look better if you carry them."

Bethany took them without speaking. Everything was strange. This was another world, a world she didn't understand. As she didn't understand this man who motioned her to follow him with a jerk of his head.

They found a room in a house a short distance from the market. It was a small room with two hammocks, a crude table, and no bathroom.

"The facilities are at the back of the house," Tiger told her.

Bethany didn't answer. She put the things Tiger had bought down on the table and moved to the hammock. All she wanted to do was close her eyes and pretend she was somewhere else.

"Mrs. Weng will give us dinner," Tiger said.

"I'll just have some fruit."

He shook his head. "You need hot food. Come along, don't argue."

Bethany glared at him, but she had no choice. For as long as this trip lasted she had to do as he said. But when this was over, when they found the dragon, she'd tell Tiger what she thought of him.

She had no idea what she ate for dinner. Once, in a low voice, she asked, "What *is* this?" and Tiger replied, "Better not ask." She made herself eat most of it, choking it down with green tea. God, how she hated green tea! If she ever got out of China she'd never have a cup of green tea for as long as she lived.

Because there were no lights, the woman of the house gave them a kerosene lantern. "I'll bring some water in so we can bathe," Tiger said as they made their way to their room. He hesitated. "Would you like me to go with you out to the yard?"

"No thank you," Bethany said coolly. "I can find my way."

Tiger handed her the lantern. She held it aloft and resolutely made her way out of the house. The yard was dark, there was no moon to light her way. She stood for a moment, not knowing which way to go, then spotted a well-worn path. There, behind what looked like a lilac bush, she found a crude wooden structure. The facilities, she thought grimly.

When Bethany returned to the room Tiger took the lantern and left. He returned a few minutes later with a bucket of water, a piece of soap, and a towel. Silently he and Bethany undressed, she with her back to him. She bathed, put on her nightgown, and turned to the hammock.

She'd never slept in a hammock before and wasn't even sure how to get in one. Tentatively she sat on the edge. The other side rose in the air, almost throwing her out.

"Sit in the middle," Tiger said, "then swing your feet up."

Bethany tried it. Half on and half off she lay back and closed her eyes. She heard Tiger's footsteps cross to her and did not open her eyes.

"We must talk," he said.

"I'm tired."

"I know you are, but this is necessary."

Bethany opened her eyes.

"You were shocked by what happened today, by the way I handled the man who had been following me."

"You could have killed him."

"No, I knew what I was doing."

"Because you've done it before?"

"Damn it, Bethany..." Tiger ran a tired hand through his black hair, then dropped to the floor beside her. "I've been expecting somebody to follow me from the time I left Tsingyun. After the attempt to kidnap you I knew we were being watched, that we would continue to be watched until we made some kind of a move. That's why I didn't want you with me. If the men who were after the dragon followed me then you would be safe. But you were determined to come with me, Bethany, and I am not sure whether it was because you wanted to be with me or because you didn't trust me."

"Not that," she said. "Never that."

Tiger went on as though he hadn't heard her. "What happened this morning was inevitable. I knew I would be followed, I knew there would be a confrontation. I didn't want you to see it."

"You would have killed him," Bethany said again. "I saw your face. I—"

"He had information I needed." Tiger's voice was cold. "He will go back to the man who sent him, to Weng Tsan Tsi. But don't think that because he has gone that another won't take his place. From now on we must watch every move we make. We must be ready to escape if escape is possible, to stand and fight if it is not. I didn't want you to come but you are here and I can't send you back." His voice tightened. "This morning I asked you to do whatever I told you to do. You disobeyed me, but you can't disobey me again. Both of our lives might depend on your obedience." He took her hand. "On your trust."

Bethany looked at him for a long moment. Then she took her hand away. "I'll do whatever you say," she said, "for as long as we are in China. But when this is over... it will be over."

Tiger sat back on his heels. "As you wish, Bethany."

Then he stood up and went to the other hammock. But it was a long time before Tiger slept that night. He knew he had been rough on Bethany and that she had been shocked by the day's events. Even as his hands had gripped his pursuer's throat this morning he'd been aware of Bethany's shocked gasp, the look of horror on her face.

Tiger closed his eyes. This was a dangerous game they were playing, she had to realize that. She wasn't in Ohio, she was in China. A lot of money was involved, money that men would kill for.

His mother had said that men had killed and been killed for the golden dragon. Tiger knew now that it was true. He knew too that he would have to be tough and resilient if he and Bethany were to come through this unscathed. He'd have given his soul to know that she was safely back in Tsingyun with his mother. And he knew that he would give his life to protect her.

With a sigh Tiger closed his eyes. Suddenly, for a reason he couldn't explain, he thought about the legend of the girl who had been Flowering Peach, and of her lover, the young poet who was turned into a dragon.

"The golden dragon is a symbol of love," his mother had said. "A love that will last forever."

Of a lost love. Tiger took a deep breath. He wanted to go to Bethany. He wanted to take her in his arms and tell her he loved her. That if the dragon was going to come between them he didn't want it—he only wanted her.

But Tiger didn't go to her. Instead he closed his eyes and thought of the next day's journey.

Chapter 14

Tiger was not in the room when Bethany awoke the next morning. She yawned, stretched, then made the mistake of rolling over...and rolled right out of the hammock. She was still on the floor, trying to gather her wits, when Tiger opened the door.

"What happened?" He put a package on the table. "Are you hurt?"

Bethany looked up at him as she ran a hand through her tousled hair. "I fell out of bed, I mean out of the hammock. I just turned over and the next thing I knew I was on the floor."

Suppressing a smile, Tiger helped her up. "Did you hurt yourself?"

"No." Bethany stepped away from him. "What time is it?"

"A little past seven. I've arranged a ride to Wenzhou. We have to leave at eight."

"In a truck?"

Tiger nodded. "But this time we ride in the front."
He handed her the package. "I bought you a cheongsam. I thought it would be cooler than the pants and
jacket you've been wearing. You must still wear the
hat of course."

Bethany opened the package and removed the dark-
blue Chinese dress. Tiger was right, it would be cooler
than the pants and jacket.

"Thank you." Her voice was still formal and withdrawn. "That was thoughtful of you."

"And here's a thermos of hot tea. I'm afraid that's
all we have time for."

"Green tea." Bethany sighed as she opened the
thermos and filled the cup.

"We can have the fruit and bread later, on the
truck. Wenzhou is less than a hundred miles from
here. Once we're there we'll get a train to take us to
Hangzhou, then on to Nanjing." Tiger hesitated. He
wanted to tell her how he felt, how he didn't want it to
be like this at all. He knew it was difficult for her. He'd
try to make it as easy for her, but he had to be strong
and make Bethany strong or they'd never come
through this.

Instead he told her not to take too long dressing,
and that he'd be waiting outside.

The cheongsam was tight across her bust, but aside
from that it fitted. Bethany applied her makeup, tied
her hair back and put on the coolie hat. Just before she
snapped her mirror shut she looked into it again, into
the face of a stranger.

"I'm Bethany Adams," she whispered to the mirror. "I'm twenty-four years old and I live in Tiffin,

Ohio." She took a deep breath. "I'm an American," she said.

The rain started an hour after they were on the road. Tiger and the driver sat in the front of the cab; Bethany sat behind them on a jump seat next to the suitcase. Tiger and the other man talked. Bethany looked out of the window at the rain.

The road was rutted, and the rain only made it worse. They passed through several villages similar to the one where she and Tiger had spent the night. There was almost no traffic on the road, only an occasional handcart and one or two bicycles. Bethany ate an orange and tried to sleep.

By the time they reached Wenzhou the rain had slowed. Tiger asked directions to the railroad station, then said to Bethany, "We will ask if there is a train to Chinhai this afternoon."

Bethany waited while he went to the ticket window to inquire. There were only a few people in the musty-smelling station: a woman with a red-cheeked baby, a husband and wife with a little boy who watched Bethany's every move, and a young man in a blue coolie suit and Mao cap who glanced away when Bethany looked at him.

When Tiger returned he said, "We're in luck. The train for Chinhai leaves in an hour. We'll spend the night there and take the train for Hangzhou and Nanjing in the morning."

Bethany nodded without speaking.

"We have time to find a restaurant and have lunch," he said. "Or if you prefer we can eat the fruit and bread I bought yesterday."

"The fruit and bread will be fine." Bethany glanced up at him as she spoke.

"Keep your head down," Tiger warned in a low voice. He took the fruit and buns out of the straw bag she carried, casually glancing around the room as he did, past the woman with the child, the husband and wife, the young man in the Mao cap whose nose was peeling from a fading sunburn.

Tiger handed Bethany a pear and said, "I'm going to buy a newspaper."

Bethany nodded without speaking. She felt curiously enervated; she didn't want to eat or move or think. It was as though all of this strangeness and the difficulties with Tiger had suddenly become too much for her to cope with. She was bereft, tired in mind and her body, and very, very alone.

"You're not eating," Tiger said when he returned.

"I'm not hungry."

"At least have some fruit."

Bethany took a bite out of the pear.

When they boarded the train the young man in the Mao cap followed them into soft class. Tiger continued reading the newspaper, preoccupied with the thought of the monsoon and that in another day or two he and Bethany would have to find a boat to make the trip up the Yangtze to Chungtai. If there was a storm the trip would have to be delayed. That thought didn't please him. He wanted to get this over with as soon as he could. Maybe when he and Bethany had the golden dragon and were on their way back to Hong Kong things would be better between them.

Tiger thought of how it had been on the boat, of the long love-filled nights, of the sunny days... Suddenly his back stiffened. Sunny days! The young man who had boarded when they did had a sunburned nose. That was strange, as there hadn't been much sun in this part of China for the past week or two. At any rate the Chinese weren't sun worshippers like the Americans or the Europeans. When they went out they wore hats to protect them from the sun. Even fishermen who spent their lives on the water usually had a protective canvas to shade them from the sun. But a man on a pleasure craft—like the craft that had pursued them on their journey to China—didn't worry about exposure to the sun.

Was this young man in his Mao cap one of the men who had pursued them?

Tiger debated about telling Bethany, and decided he wouldn't. She was having a difficult time coping; he didn't want to add to her worries. And very likely he was jumping to a false conclusion. But just in case, he'd keep an eye on the young man.

It was late afternoon when the train chugged into Chinhai. It had been raining for over a hour and as Tiger and Bethany walked through the small station they saw that the rain had increased. Tiger looked around. The young man was nowhere in sight. He felt a momentary sense of relief, sure now that he'd been wrong, that his imagination had been working over-time.

"Wait here," he told Bethany. "I will ask about a hotel and see if I can arrange for a taxi or a pedicab." He put the suitcase and the basket of food at the foot of a pillar.

Bethany nodded without speaking, tightening her hands on the small case she carried as she watched

Tiger disappear in a crowd near the door. She hoped tonight they would be in a hotel with a bed. Two beds. She was bone weary and discouraged. All she wanted was a cup of tea, even green tea, a hot shower, and a bed. She—

"Excuse me." The young man with the Mao cap stood in front of her. In careful English he said, "Your husband asked me to tell you he has a taxi waiting." He picked up the suitcase and the basket and started back into the station.

"Wait," Bethany said. "Where are you going?"

"Your husband is at the rear door, madame." He smiled a youthful smile. "The rain has worsened, he did not want you to get unduly wet."

Bethany looked around uncertainly. "My...my husband told me to wait here."

"But the cab is waiting around the corner. If you do not come it will go away. Your husband said that you must hurry, that is why he sent me to get you, rather than leave the cab."

"All right." Bethany nodded. "Let's go." Her heels tapped on the cement floor of the now empty station. She looked beyond the young man, hoping to see Tiger waiting for her at the entrance. But the entrance was empty. She peered out into the rain. A gray car was parked at the curb but there was no sign of a taxi.

Bethany turned to the young man. "Where...?" she started to say, then gasped as he grabbed her arm and shoved her toward the car. She whirled around and cried out, trying desperately to break away from him. But it was too late. The back door of the car swung open. She was thrust inside, the young man jumped in behind her, the tires screeched and the car pulled away from the curb.

Because of the rain it took Tiger longer than he expected to find a cab. He went two blocks before he found one and when he did he said, "I want to go to a hotel, a good one."

"I know the best. I will take you there."

"First we must go back to the station. My wife is waiting there because of the rain." Tiger got into the cab and closed the door. When the driver pulled into the station entrance Tiger got out. "I will be only a moment," he said.

Tiger ran through the rain into the empty station. He stopped, at first bewildered, then angry because Bethany wasn't where he had left her. He stood for a moment, uncertain. Where had she gone? Where in the hell...? Then a cold knot of fear formed in his stomach and he raced forward, uncertain, frantically searching the now empty station. Then, at the back, he saw a flash of blue. A blue cheongsam, a blue cap.

Though he was halfway into the station, Tiger could see out the door. He saw the gray car and heard the screech of tires, and a fear such as he'd never known before clutched at his insides. With a muttered oath he turned and sprinted back the way he had come. When he reached the cab he threw open the door and shouted, "Around the corner. A gray car. Follow it!"

"But sir..."

Tiger threw a wad of money into the front seat. "Follow that car!" he shouted.

Tires screeched as the cab driver gunned forward, spun on two wheels around the corner, righted. Ahead through the rain Tiger saw the car. "Bethany!" his mind screamed. "Bethany!"

The young man holding her wrists yelled something to the driver, who stepped sharply on the gas, skidding wildly as he rounded a corner. Bethany screamed and he said, "Shut up!"

She tried to break away and he struck her a blow on the side of her head that dazed her. He looked behind him, swore, then leaning toward the front, shouted again at the driver. They rounded another corner, passed a green-roofed pagoda, entered a market section. The street narrowed. An old man with a pushcart stepped from the curb. Face frozen with fear, he saw the gray car and jumped back out of the way. The car smashed into the cart, as fruits and vegetables flew up over the hood of the car and out onto the street.

Bethany's captor released her to lean over the front seat and scream at the driver. She huddled in the corner of the car, hanging on to a strap, bracing her feet on the floor boards. Suddenly ahead of her she saw a pedicab swerve into the street. Horror stricken she watched as the man driving it saw the gray car. Even through the rain she could see his eyes widen in fear.

The driver yelled out in frustration as the car swerved. He missed the man by inches, but not the pedicab. It flew up into the air, over the hood, as the car careened wildly, out of control. The young man in the blue cap screamed. The driver fought to control the car.

Bethany was thrown to the floor when the car bounced up over the curb, through a row of fruit stands, and slammed into a low wooden structure.

The car came to a stop. She sat up. Her captor lay half over the front seat, feet dangling, silent. The driver moaned, then said something Bethany didn't understand or didn't wait to hear. Her hand was on the door handle, she rolled out of the car and staggered to her feet.

People appeared in the street. They pointed at the car, they shouted at her.

She stood there, dazed, disoriented, as a taxi screeched to a stop.

"Bethany!" Tiger ran toward her. He grabbed her arms. "Are you all right, Bethany?" he cried. "Answer me!"

"Yes, I . . ." She sagged in his arms.

Tiger picked her up. He ran back to the taxi and put her inside, then ran back to the gray car. The young man he'd seen on the train lay sprawled over the front seat. Tiger reached in, found his wrist, and knew the man was dead. The driver was unconscious. Tiger hesitated only a moment before he went back to his taxi. "Let's get out of here," he said tersely.

His driver looked pale and shaken. "Yes, it is better not to wait for questions from the police." He backed up the car, drove cautiously around the crash scene, then sped off.

Tiger took hold of Bethany's shoulders so that he could look at her. She had a small cut on her cheek and her eyes were dazed. She'd lost the coolie hat.

"That man," she managed to say. "The one with the blue hat. He told me you'd sent him to get me. He said you were waiting with a cab. It was the young man from the train. I thought it was all right...I know you told me to wait and that you're angry, but..." She began to weep.

"Don't cry," Tiger said as he drew her into his arms. "It's all right, Bethany. I'm not angry. It wasn't your fault. All that matters is that you're all right."

"Do you want to go the hotel now?" the driver asked nervously.

Tiger hesitated. If there were others here in Chenhai who were associated with the men who had tried to kidnap Bethany, the first place they would look would be in a hotel. He couldn't risk it. "No," he said, "not a hotel. Do you know of a guest house, someone who would rent a room? I would pay very well."

"My wife and I have an extra room." The driver looked doubtful. "But my house is humble, perhaps it would not be suitable."

"It will be suitable." Tiger looked out of the back window; no car was following them. "I would consider it a great favor if you and your wife would allow us to stay with you."

"Then it is done." The driver slowed to a circumspect speed as Tiger settled back in the seat. Bethany had stopped crying but when she tried to move away from him, Tiger put his arm around her and drew her closer. He remembered the way he had felt when he went back into the station and Bethany wasn't there. He'd gone hollow inside, afraid for a moment that she had run away from him. Then when rational thinking had taken over, fear clutched at him and he'd raced toward the other exit in time to see her being shoved into a car.

His arm tightened around her shoulders. He knew that if the man who had taken her hadn't already been dead that he would have killed him.

The cabdriver's house was at the end of an unpaved street. It was a square, box-shaped house, flat against the house next to it, with a fenced-in dirt yard in the front and chicken coops in the back. The front door opened. A tall woman dressed in a brown coolie jacket and pants came out into the yard. Her hair and eyebrows were streaked with gray. She had laugh lines around her eyes and mouth and when she smiled showed two silver teeth.

The driver said something to her. She listened, then bowed and said something Bethany didn't understand.

"Mrs. Li says that we are welcome," Tiger told Bethany. He took her arm and led her into the house behind the still smiling woman.

The room she showed them to was small but clean. There was a window, a straw mattress in one corner, a table and one chair. She said something else and bowed herself out of the room.

"Mrs. Li will prepare dinner for us," Tiger said as Bethany sat down on the chair.

"I don't think I can eat."

"You haven't eaten all day."

"I'm sorry about the suitcase. We've lost everything. All of our clothes..." She tried to tuck a strand of her hair under the kerchief.

"It doesn't matter. Tomorrow I will buy other things."

"If I had done as you said—"

Tiger took her hands. "It's my fault. I suspected the young man and I didn't tell you because I didn't want you to worry." His hands gripped her. "It would have been my fault if anything had happened to you, Bethany. When I saw him shove you into the car I..." He stopped, unable to go on. "I won't let you out of my sight again," he said finally. "Not for a minute."

A little while later Mrs. Li knocked at their door and led them into a small kitchen where she had prepared bean curd with egg, flat bread, and noodles mixed with dried fish. For the first time since Bethany had started on the trip she found that she was hungry. She ate everything that was served and even drank the green tea without complaint.

Mrs. Li watched her while she ate.

With her gaze still on Bethany she spoke to Tiger. He answered her and to Bethany he said in English, "She wanted to know if you were English. I told her your mother was English but your father was Chinese and that you live in Hong Kong." He frowned. "I'm afraid we will have to do something about your hair tomorrow."

"Like what?" Bethany said.

"I think we will have to cut it, Bethany. And if it is possible, we should color it."

Bethany touched the kerchief that bound her hair and stared at Tiger. Cut her hair? Color it?

When the meal was finished and Mrs. Li and Tiger had each bowed several times, he and Bethany retired to their small room. By the dim light of the naked overhead light, her back to Tiger, Bethany undressed. Because she had no gown she pulled her half-slip up over her breasts and folded the blue cheongsam over the chair. Without looking at Tiger she knelt on the straw mattress and moved as close to the wall as she could get.

Tiger didn't speak as he turned out the light. She felt his weight on the mattress and held her breath.

"This has been a difficult day for you," Tiger said into the silence of the room. "Try to sleep now."

Bethany closed her eyes. She felt so very tired. She shifted to a more comfortable position, stifling a groan when she discovered a bruise on her hip she didn't know she had. Her whole body had begun to ache from the jolt she'd suffered when the car had come to a crashing halt. At last she relaxed, but close to the edge of sleep she jerked awake. The vision of the young man in the blue Mao cap hanging lifelessly across the front seat seared her mind's eye. All the horror of her kidnapping, the wild chase through the streets and the crash, came rushing back.

"What is it?" Tiger asked.

"Nothing, I . . ." Involuntarily Bethany shuddered.

"You have every right to be frightened by what happened today," he said as he reached for her hand.

For a moment Bethany stiffened and tried to draw her hand away. But when he said, "Come, let me hold you," she didn't resist. Instead, scarcely knowing what she was doing, seeking only the security of his arms, Bethany clung to him. Burying her face in the hollow between his shoulder and throat, she burrowed closer, trying to blot out the terrible experiences of the day.

Tiger stroked the length of her back, calming her fears, soothing her to quietness. Without thinking Bethany pressed her body close to his. He could feel her warmth and her softness as she trembled against him, and felt the urgency of need rise in his body. He tried to suppress it, knowing this was not the time, knowing that Bethany needed only the comfort of his arms. But oh God, how he wanted her!

Bethany knew. Suddenly, through her fear, she became aware of Tiger's urgency and it was as though she stopped, hesitated, and shifted from fear into awareness, then to awakening desire.

She kissed the hollow of his throat as his arms tightened around her, then lifted her face for his kiss. With the kiss all the tension of the day and all of the angry words that had passed between them vanished. She was safe in Tiger's arms, enveloped by the warmth of his body.

"Bethany," he breathed against her lips. He cupped her breasts and ran his fingertips over the ready peaks, shaking with pleasure when she whispered his name.

Tension, anger and danger were forgotten. They were lost in each other, their breathing quickening as they waited for the moment when their bodies would be joined.

Tiger seared a path of kisses down her throat. He nuzzled her ear and told her that he loved her. Bethany clasped his shoulders and uttered little cries of delight as he caressed her with his hands and his mouth. One hand traveled down and across her stomach. He touched her gently, teased and excited her until it became more than either of them could bear.

"Tiger," she whispered. "Oh, Tiger, please."

He came up over her then. "Yes," he answered. "Yes, love, now."

This is the way that wounds are healed, Bethany thought as she gave herself up to the sheer pleasure of the moment. This is all that matters, this closeness we share, this joy that goes beyond description. She lifted her body to his. Her fingers threaded through the thick black hair as she matched the cadence of his strokes and wondered if anything could ever be this wonderful again. Would she ever be this alive again? Every nerve tingled with excitement as she moved still closer to him.

Tiger rocked her body in time with his, whispering words of love. He leaned to take one rigid nipple between his teeth and an electric shock of pleasure shot through Bethany. She gasped his name and turned her face into his shoulder as her world exploded into a shimmering kaleidoscope of color and feeling. Tiger's arms came around her. He sought her mouth and cried the joy of his fulfillment against her lips.

They held each other, heart beating against heart, as he soothed her to calmness and told her how beautiful and brave she was.

A straw-filled mattress in a small and simple room, Bethany thought as she drifted off to sleep in Tiger's arms. But it's home, my home because Tiger is here. Because I love him.

Chapter 15

A man and a woman had entered the house of Mrs. Li the day before. A man and a boy left the house the next afternoon. The boy wore a navy-blue cotton coolie outfit and soft black slippers. A blue Mao cap covered his hair.

Bethany hadn't protested that morning when Tiger sat her in the chair in their room and told her he had to cut her hair. She'd clenched her hands in her lap as she looked up at him, her gray eyes wide with appeal. "Isn't there any other way?" she'd asked.

"I'm afraid not." He held her head straight and began to cut with scissors he'd borrowed from Mrs. Li. Handfuls of golden-blond hair fell to the floor. Bethany closed her eyes. She knew that Tiger was right, this had to be done, but that didn't mean she had to like it.

Tiger went on until her neck felt cold and bare, then stopped, tilted her face up, and began to trim around her face. Bangs fell across her forehead and he brushed them back with his fingers.

"That will do," Tiger said as he looked at her with a face as strained as her own. "Now we will color it."

Choking back words of protest, she leaned over a bucket of water and closed her eyes while Tiger shampooed her hair with the black tint he had purchased that morning.

He knew she hated this as much as he hated doing it, but they had no choice. The same men who had attacked Bethany in his mother's courtyard in Tsingyun, the men who had followed them to the South China Sea, were still looking for them. Even though one of them had been killed yesterday, there would be others to take his place. They had to move carefully. The disguise would give them a measure of protection, a protection they desperately needed.

When Bethany's hair was dry Tiger handed her a mirror and led her to the window. "You look different," he said in a low voice, "but you are still beautiful."

She looked into the mirror. Someone with shaggy, boyishly cropped black hair looked back at her. "It's awful," she said in a shocked voice. "I look awful."

Tiger put his arms around her and before she could speak he led her to the chair, sat down, and pulled her onto his lap. "It would be impossible for you to look awful." He tilted her chin up so that he could kiss her as he stroked the back of her neck. "You feel sleek and sexy," he whispered.

"I don't feel sexy." Bethany pulled away from him. "I feel naked."

One black eyebrow rose. "Really? How nice." He pulled the half-slip that covered her down to her waist.

"Tiger!" she protested. But the protest died on her lips when he kissed her breasts. "It's late," she whispered against the thickness of his hair. "We don't have time."

"We'll always have time." He picked her up and carried her to the straw-filled bed. "We'll always make time." Gently he lowered her and stripped the slip and the panties down over her ankles. "You have lovely legs," he said, looking down at her as he stepped out of his trousers. "When this is over, when we are back in Hong Kong, you must never again wear pants. I want to see you in short swirling skirts and high heels." He kissed the back of her knee and felt her shiver as he began to trail a line of kisses up her thighs.

Bethany gasped. "Tiger, please . . ."

"Please what, Bethany?" He nipped her tender skin and softly caressed it with his tongue before he moved up over her to kiss her breasts. He held her close while he kissed her and stroked the back of her slender neck. He wanted to tell her that she was still beautiful and that he loved her. But he didn't tell her with words, he told her with the way he held her and by the touch of his hands.

I adore you, his hands said. I love the feel of your skin beneath my fingertips, the warmth of your body close to mine. I love your determination and your bravery, and yes, I even love your stubbornness. He sought her lips and when they parted beneath his he sighed against them. She put her arms around him and he knew it was time—it was past time.

Gently, almost reverently, Tiger joined his body to Bethany's, holding her close, making them one. As his body began to move against hers Tiger knew that he would never tire of loving her. Bethany lifted her body to his and Tiger groaned with pleasure. She murmured a litany of love and his body tightened and trembled.

"My love," he whispered against her throat. "My love."

Tiger felt the frantic beat of her heart, the tightening of her muscles as she moaned his name. His body shook in a paroxysm of pleasure. He clung to Bethany, knowing that if he didn't he would rocket into space. He cupped her face with his hands. He kissed her, ravaging her mouth with his tongue, still in the throes of passion, never wanting it to end.

At last Tiger held her in the crook of his arm, seeking calmness, feeling the rapid thud of his heart against his chest. I love her, he thought. With her I feel a depth of passion I have never felt before. She is all I want, all I will ever want. And suddenly he knew that the golden dragon had lost its importance. He didn't need it; all he needed in this world was Bethany's love.

Tiger tilted her face up to his. "Let's go home, Bethany," he said. "Let's go back to Hong Kong."

Her gray eyes widened. "Go back to Hong Kong? What do you mean? What about the dragon?"

"We don't need it, Bethany. I have enough money. We can live comfortably on what I make from the club. We don't need—"

"I do." Bethany pulled away from him and sat up. "I need the dragon. My father and your father wanted us to have it. We've risked our lives for it. We can't stop now. I *won't* stop now." She shook her head. "We've come so far, Tiger. We can't give up now."

Tiger looked at her for a long moment. He took a deep breath and let it out slowly. "You know how dangerous it can be. And still you insist on continuing?"

Bethany lifted her chin. "Yes, Tiger, I insist."

He looked at her for a long moment. "Then we'll continue," he said. "And God help us both."

The train left Chinhai at three o'clock that afternoon, past temples and pagodas, past bedclothes airing on bamboo poles from whitewashed houses, over stone bridges out to rolling hills and a countryside green with summer. There were few people in soft class, and none of them paid any attention to the tall man or the boy with him. If they did they assumed the boy was a younger brother making his first trip on a train, for he kept his face turned away from the other passengers to look out at the passing landscape.

It was after dark when Bethany and Tiger arrived in Hangzhou. The train for Nanjing would not leave until seven the next morning. They spent the night in a small hotel near the railway station.

"I look like a boy," Bethany said when she looked at herself in the mirror over the dresser of their hotel room.

"Then take off your clothes so I'll know you're a woman." Tiger smiled at her.

"A woman who needs a shower." She frowned at herself in the mirror. "I don't look like me anymore, do I?"

"You are you," Tiger said. "Whatever the color of your hair or your skin. Now go and take your shower and when you are finished we will lie together and I will tell you how beautiful I think you are."

Bethany's face softened. She took his hand. "Come shower with me," she said. "We'll bathe each other."

Hand in hand they stepped into the shower. Carefully, tenderly, they washed each other's bodies. Hands lingered over curves and planes, hesitated over places of pleasure, kissed and clung while the water cascaded over them. When it became too much, they stepped out and quickly dried each other.

They had a bed this time, a bed with a mattress that sloped and sagged in the middle. But that didn't matter; Bethany had come home once more to the warmth of Tiger's arms.

At the station the next morning they drank hot tea and ate rolls stuffed with meat and mushrooms. Again, as she had the day before, Bethany kept her head lowered and the cap pulled down over her eyes. From time to time, without thinking, her fingers touched the back of her neck. She felt exposed, and wondered if her hair would ever grow long again.

"Do you think . . . ?" she started to ask Tiger, then stopped. He was pretending to read a newspaper, but his eyes were narrowed as he scanned every waiting passenger.

Bethany swallowed as she felt the fear that was by now so familiar creep into her body. She saw Tiger stiffen and lower his head as a voice called out over the loudspeaker. "Come," he said, "they're calling our train."

She wanted to look around to find whatever it was that he thought spelled danger. Instead she picked up the new wicker basket that held their few belongings and followed him down the track. They boarded the train, she a few steps behind him. Two men, a man and a woman, and a single man boarded behind them.

When they found their seats Tiger spoke to her in Chinese, his voice impatient, an older brother speaking to his younger brother. Then leaning closer to her whispered in English, "Take whatever you need from the basket and put it in your pockets. Soon the train will begin to move out of the yard. When I speak to you again I want you to get up and walk back to the door. Don't hurry. Just act naturally."

He turned away from her, took a newspaper from the basket, and began to read.

Bethany stared straight ahead, too frightened to speak. The door of the train clanged shut. A voice rang out. She took the dark makeup, eyeliner, a comb and the scarf out of the basket. Steam hissed, the train began to move out through the yard, chugging slowly, past freight cars, signalmen, and workers with lunch pails. Rain spattered the windows as the train began to pick up speed. They were on the outskirts of the town, passing a wooded area.

"Now." The word was so low Bethany could barely hear it. Her mouth was dry, her palms wet. She stood up, and with her head lowered walked slowly to the back of the train. Suddenly Tiger shot around her. He pulled the door open and shoved her out onto the swaying platform.

A shout rang out in the car behind them as Tiger jerked the handle of the platform door and kicked it open. Wind and rain blew in.

The door behind them started to open. Tiger put his foot against it. Bethany saw a man with a gun, his face twisted with anger as he put his shoulder to the door.

"Jump!" Tiger ordered.

Bethany felt a hand in the middle of her back. She screamed, then hurtled through space. The ground came up to meet her. She fell, rolled, and came to a thudding stop against the trunk of a tree.

Bruised, dazed, the breath almost knocked out of her, Bethany stood on shaky legs and clung to the tree for support. She shook her head, trying to get her bearings. Everything had happened so fast. The open door, the ground rushing by, the man with a gun... Tiger! her mind screamed. Where was he? Oh, my God, what if he was still on the train? What if he was wounded or...?

The train chugged farther down the track. As Bethany watched, she saw him leap from the train, hit the ground and roll.

With a strangled cry Bethany ran toward him.

Tiger stood up, waved and began running toward her through the slanting rain. "Are you all right?" he cried when he reached her. He grabbed her shoulders, then moved down her arms to her hands, as though assuring himself that no bones were broken. He touched her face. "You've got a nasty scratch," he said.

"I haven't had much practice jumping off trains." Bethany attempted a smile.

"It was a terrible thing to do to you, but I wasn't sure until we were on the train that the man I spotted watching us in the station was on to us." Tiger pushed the rain-damp hair back from his face. "After you jumped I wrestled the gun out of his hand and knocked him down—that's what took me so long."

"They're trying to kill us," Bethany said. "But that doesn't make sense, Tiger. We know where the dragon is; if they kill us they lose the dragon."

"Not us, Bethany. *Me.* It's me they want out of the way because they think they'll be able to force you to lead them to the statue." Tiger put his hands on her shoulders. "That's why they tried to kidnap you that night in Tsingyun, and that's why they forced you into the car the other day."

"You're scaring me," she said.

"Good, I want you to be scared. I want you to know how serious this is." Tiger looked around. "We've got to find shelter. Come on, let's head for that stand of trees."

But first they went back to where she had landed to find her cap. By that time the rain had slowed to a mean, misty drizzle. Heavy gray clouds hung low in the sky and a cold wind blew through the trees. They walked for over an hour before they found a deserted shed.

"I suppose we'll have to take what shelter we can find," Tiger said. "Let's try it."

The walls were made of mud brick. A broken half-door hung on one rusted hinge. But inside the shed was warm and dry. The smell, not unpleasant of animals that may have once sheltered there, clung to the straw strewn on the rough wooden floor.

"We'll spend the night here." Tiger looked around. "Tomorrow morning we'll try to find a road and transportation."

Bethany nodded as she sank down on a pile of straw, accepting the arrangement without complaint. So much had happened to her since she'd left home that spending the night in a deserted barn almost seemed normal.

When it grew dark the rain began again, slapping hard against the straw roof. They leaned their backs against the rough wall of the barn. Tiger put his arms around Bethany. They talked of many things, but not about the golden dragon.

He thought that now, after today, they might have lost their pursuers. That's why he'd gotten on the train, although he suspected one of the men in the station might be after them. He and Bethany would stay away from the larger cities and they'd try to take a boat from somewhere along the Yangtze rather than from Nanjing. No one knew they were headed for Chungtai. If they could get there without any more trouble they'd be home free.

Tiger rested his chin against the top of Bethany's head. We will get the dragon, he thought. We will return to Tsingyun by a different route, and when we have rested we will go home. Home to Hong Kong.

When morning came they walked across the still damp fields until they found a road, and finally a man with an ox cart. Tiger explained that he and his younger brother, who could not speak, were on their way to the Yangtze River basin. He also said they'd had no food since the day before and that he would be glad to pay for whatever the man could offer them and for a ride in the cart. The man dug into his knapsack, drew out two pears and a few chestnuts, and gestured to the back of the cart.

It was a morning Bethany knew she would always remember. The sky was clear, the countryside washed clean by the rain. Her body was stiff and sore from the fall she'd taken the day before. But she was alive, the sun shone on her face, and she was with Tiger.

Late that night they arrived at a farm on the outskirts of Nanjing. The man with the cart, happy with the money Tiger had paid him for the ride and the food, said, "My farm is humble, but there is room if you want to sleep here for the night. My wife will give you supper."

"We would be most honored," Tiger said as he helped Bethany out of the cart. "But please let me pay for our lodging."

That night, by the light of one flickering candle, they ate rice and vegetables in a thick black bean sauce. It was a simple meal, served on two cracked plates, but it was wonderful. Later the farmer's wife gave them a candle and showed them to their room.

It was filled with sacks of grain and baskets of onions. In one corner there was a rolled-up straw mat.

"That's our bed." Tiger shook his head. "I'm sorry, Bethany, but I'm afraid this it for tonight." He put the candle on the floor.

"A hard bed is supposed to be good for your back," Bethany said as she stretched. "It's warm and it's dry and I like the smell of onions." She went to stand by the open window. "It's so quiet," she whispered. "I never knew any place could be this quiet."

Tiger stood beside her, his arm around her waist, unable for a moment to speak. He held her close and together they looked out at the dark, silent, sweet-smelling night.

Chapter 16

Tiger and Bethany found a raft loaded with timber on its way to a sawmill in Chungtai at the village of Tungling. At first the boatman, a scrawny man in his seventies, shook his head. "No," he said, "I cannot take passengers."

"I will pay you well." Tiger took money from his pocket. "Enough to keep you and your family for a year."

But still the man hesitated. "You can take a river steamer from Nanjing. Why would you want to take my raft?"

"We are not in Nanjing, we are in Tungling. You have a motor on your raft. With it you will make better time than the steamer because you will not have to slow through the gorges."

"On the steamer you would have a cabin." The old man gestured to a bamboo lean-to. "That will be your accommodation on my raft."

"It will do very well for my brother and me." Tiger reached into his pocket again. "Now you have enough money to keep you for the next two years," he said.

"You must want to get to Chungtai very badly." The boatman pocketed the money.

"How long will the trip take?"

"Two or three days, depending on the currents. Come then, if you are coming, I am ready to cast off."

"Very well, and thank you." Tiger looked at Bethany. With a nod of his head he motioned her onto the raft, taking from her the basket of fruit and bottled water they had bought that morning.

Keeping her head down, Bethany nodded to the boatman and went to sit in front of the lean-to.

The morning was pleasantly warm; the water was smooth. Bethany had read about the Yangtze, but it was hard to believe that she was here, about to embark on a trip up the longest river in Asia.

There was a never ending panorama of life along the great river. Hour by hour the landscape unfolded before them. There was endless traffic too—other rafts, some of them carrying passengers and produce, junks with red sails taut in the breeze, sampans, barges, a passenger steamer.

Most of the time Tiger stood beside the boatman. His face was thoughtful, pensive. Their journey had almost come to an end. Tomorrow, or the day after, they would be in Chungtai. He was sure now that they had lost the men who had been pursuing them. There was a chance someone would watch the stops along the Yangtze where passenger steamers docked, but it would be impossible for them to observe all of the traffic on this three-thousand-mile river.

Even if somehow the men followed them to Chung-tai they could never know about the monastery. He and Bethany would go there as soon as they arrived in the city. Then the golden dragon would be theirs.

Tiger's hand tightened around the keys in his pocket, the keys that would unlock the secret of the dragon. Finding it was not as important to him as it had once been. He had a bad feeling about the dragon now; he'd had it ever since that night in the garden when his mother had told Bethany and himself about the warlord and his son. The golden dragon was a symbol of love, his mother had said. Yet men had killed to possess it.

Tiger looked at Bethany. She was sitting in front of the lean-to, chin resting on her knees as she gazed out at the great river. With her hair shorn she looked very young and fragile. But he knew now that Bethany wasn't as fragile as she looked. She'd been exposed to dangers, and to a totally new culture, not the Chinese culture that tourists experienced, but the China that existed beyond the tourist hotels, the temples and the gardens. She'd slept on a bed of straw in a peasant home and on the floor of a barn without a complaint. She faced each new experience with a courage that Tiger admired more than he could ever tell her.

As he watched Bethany, Tiger thought of his love for her. He would never have known her if it hadn't been for the dragon. And he knew that, although he didn't want it, he would get it for her. He looked out over the river. He worried that after they found it Bethany would no longer need him, that she would go back to her own country where he could never follow.

For a moment Tiger felt the chill of desperation because there were times when he didn't know who he was, whether he was Chinese or American. In Hong Kong it didn't matter. He was only a man, a man who was able to enjoy what was best of both the East and of the West. But he didn't think Bethany would be happy there; a part of her would always long for the sights and sounds of her America.

At noon Tiger and Bethany sat near the lean-to while they ate the fruit they had purchased that morning. Later he fished and that evening, when the traffic on the river slowed, the boatman tied the raft to a small dock. Over a charcoal brazier the boatman cooked the fish Tiger had caught that day and triumphantly brought out two bottles of beer. Together the three of them watched the sun set over the Yungtzo, and later, while the two men talked, Bethany crawled into the lean-to and went to sleep.

Our journey is almost over, she thought as she lay looking up through cracks in the bamboo slats. The dragon is almost ours. She closed her eyes and finally, to the putt-putt rhythm of the motor, went to sleep. She dreamed of Flowering Peach and of the handsome young poet who was her lover. And as Bethany slept it seemed to her that she could hear the sad, sweet music of a lute.

On the evening of the second day they entered the placid waters near Changtai.

"It is late," the boatman said. "We will anchor here for the night. Tomorrow we will go on to Changtai."

To Changtai and the golden dragon. Tiger looked at Bethany. Our journey has almost ended, my love, he thought. Tomorrow we will find the dragon.

* * *

Changtai, on the south bank of the Yangtze, was a busy port. The old city walls, dating back to the Han Dynasty, no longer existed, but still the city, with temples and shrines, and pagodas set beside glistening lakes, had a feeling of antiquity.

"We are here at last," Tiger said as he and Bethany stepped ashore. He turned to wave to the boatman who had let them off further down the bank, away from the more commercial part of the docks. "Let's try to find a restaurant, then we will ask about the monastery." He hesitated. "Or would you like to rest today? We could find a hotel and go to the monastery tomorrow."

Bethany shook her head. As much as she longed for a bath and a change of clothes, nothing was as important as finding the dragon. "Let's go to the monastery," she said.

Almost angrily Tiger took her arm, then he looked around, trying to get his bearings. They walked for several minutes and when they found a restaurant that he thought might be acceptable, he led Bethany inside. He ordered for both of them, noodles, baked fish and hot tea, and when it was served he said, "We must talk seriously now, Bethany."

Her gray eyes regarded him suspiciously. "Yes?" She spooned up a mouthful of noodles.

"I think we've lost the men who have been following us."

"Thank goodness."

"But we must go cautiously, just in case."

Bethany nodded. "I understand."

Tiger rested his chopsticks on the side of his bowl. "Are you sure of what we're doing, Bethany?" he asked in a low voice. "Are you sure you want to go through with this?"

"Go through with it? With finding the dragon?" Her brows came together in a frown. "What are you talking about? Of course I want to go through with it. My God, Tiger, we've been through so much, we've risked so much. How can you even think of giving up when when we're this close?"

"We wouldn't be giving up, Bethany. We'd be letting go."

"I don't see the difference," she said angrily. "Our fathers risked their lives for the golden dragon, Tiger. They wanted us to have it. We can't stop now, not when we're so close."

"All right," Tiger said in a quiet voice. "If you're sure."

"I'm sure."

They ate the meal in silence, and when they were finished Tiger asked the waiter about the monastery.

"It is near Red Hill," the waiter told him. "You will pass the Endless Sky Pavilion. Just beyond the Pavilion you will see another hill in the distance. That is the Hill of Eternal Spring where the historical Museum of Oshan with its wealth of artifacts is located. To your right you will see the monastery."

Tiger thanked and paid the waiter. When they left the restaurant he said, "We'll take a taxi, but I'm not sure how we'll get back to town again." He took Bethany's arm, but still he hesitated. They were almost at their destination; why did he hesitate? In a little while the dragon, the golden dragon that men killed to own, would be theirs.

Bethany was silent on the way up into the hills. Her heart thudded with excitement as she gazed out of the taxi window. The taxi drove away from the city, then wound up the mountain to where the beauty of trees hung heavy with summer blossoms and the air was filled with summer silence.

The monastery, which stood on a peak overlooking the Yangtze, looked as though it had been hewn out of the mountain, ancient and forever, a part of the landscape that was China. The breath caught in Bethany's throat as she looked up at it. This was another world, a world she had not even dared to dream about. The early morning mist had not yet lifted from the surrounding blue-shadowed mountains. The air was clean and pure and still.

The taxi driver left them at a tall iron gate that marked the entrance. "I'll call for you in one hour," he agreed when Tiger paid him. "I'll wait at the gate. If you don't come I'll return to the city."

"In case we're not here it'll be worth your while to wait for at least thirty minutes."

The driver nodded. "Thirty minutes," he said.

When the taxi drove off Tiger stepped up to the gate and pulled a bell rope. The sound of the ancient bell reverberated in the clear morning air.

Bethany wiped her damp palms against her trousers.

A Buddhist monk in a white robe approached the gate. He bowed formally and said, "Good morning, travelers. How may I serve you?"

Tiger bowed in return. "Good morning," he said. "A long time ago my father was allowed to leave something of value here at your monastery. I have come to claim it."

"I know nothing of this, but perhaps the elders do." The monk opened the gate and stood aside for Bethany and Tiger to enter, then beckoned them to follow him.

Bethany glanced nervously around her. It's so quiet, she thought. It's as though we were at the top of the world. There was no sound except for the wind through the poplar trees and the soft slap of the monk's straw slippers.

Before their guide could knock, a door of the monastery opened and another monk motioned them inside. The first man spoke rapidly in a dialect Tiger didn't understand, then said to him, "Wait here, please."

Then they were left alone.

Bethany reached for Tiger's hand. "We're almost there," she said in a low voice.

He squeezed her hand. "Yes," he said, whispering as she had whispered, for this was a holy place. It seemed strange to him that an object that had caused so much violence should be here in this ancient, peaceful setting. Why had their fathers chosen the monastery to hide the dragon? It was so far from everything, so removed from civilization. Perhaps that was the reason. Perhaps they'd known that in this inviolate place their treasure would be safe.

Tiger looked down at Bethany. She had removed the Mao cap and stood quietly, her head bowed. He wanted to reach out and touch her. But he didn't; he only waited until the monk who had opened the door returned and said, "Follow me, please. The Saka Muni Buddha will see you now."

They were led down a long, silent hall and through an open corridor that bordered a flower-filled central patio. When they stopped before a tall, carved door, Bethany looked up at Tiger. The monk knocked. Tiger took a deep breath as the door opened.

The monk seated behind the cherry wood desk was very old. His skin looked like dried parchment, the hand that bade them enter was blue veined and wrinkled.

"My brother tells me that you have come for something that we have held for many years," he said in a thin, high voice. "I am glad that you have come, for if the object is what I think it is, it is too beautiful to hide away." He indicated two straight, high-backed chairs, and when Tiger and Bethany were seated he said, "Do you have the keys."

"Yes, Eminence." Tiger bowed, then handed over the two keys.

With a shaking hand the monk took a pair of glasses from his desk and put them on. "There were two men," he said. He looked at Bethany. "She is not Chinese. Does she understand what we are saying?"

"No, Eminence. Her father was with my father when they brought the . . . the package here."

"Yes, I remember." The monk spoke now in careful English. "There were two young men, handsome lads in the prime of their youth. Why have they not come themselves?"

"They are both dead, honored sir. We are their only heirs."

"I see." The monk took the keys Tiger had given him and slowly he got up and moved around his desk to a heavy wooden trunk bound with brass fittings. Leaning down, holding the edge of the trunk for support, he fitted the two keys into two separate locks. "Please help me," he said. "I fear the lid is too heavy for me."

Tiger moved quickly to the monk's side and opened the trunk.

The monk pointed a bony finger. "Take out the oblong box."

Carefully, scarcely daring to breath, Tiger took the box. It was heavy. He put it down, then closed the trunk. At the monk's nod, Tiger picked up the box and carried it to the desk.

"Open it," the old man said. "You must be sure."

"Yes." Tiger glanced at Bethany. She pressed trembling hands against her face.

Tiger undid the cord that bound the box. He took off the lid. The statue had been wrapped in scarlet silk. He removed it from the box and placed it on the desk. He looked at Bethany, waiting.

"Unwrap it." Her voice was husky when she spoke.

Tiger took a deep breath. The silk was soft beneath his fingertips. Slowly, carefully, he unwrapped the statue. Hardly daring to speak he freed the golden dragon from its wrapping and placed it on the desk.

He heard Bethany gasp and the ancient monk murmur. But he couldn't speak, he could only stare at the object before him.

The dragon stood almost two feet tall. More man than beast, half standing, half reclining, it was an object of ancient, priceless beauty.

"I didn't know," Bethany said in a hushed voice, "I didn't know it would be this beautiful." With a trembling hand she touched the dragon. It seemed . . . it seemed to quiver beneath her fingers. The emerald eyes seemed to look directly into her eyes. Bethany's breath stopped, her body stilled. She saw the golden tear. She passed a finger over it, then, scarcely knowing what she was doing, brought her finger to her lips—and tasted salt.

The Hotel of the Swallows was almost new. It had been built only four years before when tourists began flooding into China. At first the tourists had traveled only to the well-known cities like Beijing, Shanghai and Guangzhou. Now they came up the Yangtze River to cities like Chungtai.

There were twin beds in their fourth-floor room. There was also a cupboard for their clothes and a separate bathroom. On a table opposite the bed there was a thermos of boiled water and a tin of green tea.

Bethany sank down on one of the beds. She took off the black slippers, lay back against the pillows and closed her eyes. The taxi had not been at the gate when they left the monastery. They had waited, hoping he would come, then started the long trek down the mountain road that led to the town. Half way down they had seen the taxi chugging up.

"I was delayed," the driver explained.

"It's all right," Tiger said. "Just take us to a hotel."

Now they were here and suddenly Bethany was too tired to move. Perhaps it was the reaction, the letdown after finding the golden treasure at the end of the rainbow. She hadn't expected to feel like this; she'd expected to feel jubilant and rich. But she no longer saw the dragon in terms of dollar signs. It was an ancient object of art, of beauty and of grace.

Tiger unwrapped the dragon and placed it on the other bed. "Is it what you expected?" he asked in a low voice.

"No...no, it isn't. I've never seen anything so magnificent."

"Nor have I."

"Will it be difficult, taking it back to Tsingyun, I mean?"

"We will go by another route. But first we will rest here for a few days. I don't think that whoever has been after us will trace us to here, but it is best that we not wander around the town. One of us must be here in the room all of the time to watch the dragon."

Bethany nodded. "We should let your mother know that we've found it."

"I don't think that would be wise," Tiger said. "It's possible that someone is still watching the house in Tsingyun. I know that Mother is worried, but I don't think we should risk trying to contact her. We will be there before the week is over, then she will know that all is well." He ran his hand down the dragon's back. "It *is* beautiful, isn't it?"

"The poet," Bethany said. "Yes, he's beautiful."

Tiger looked at her. But before he could speak Bethany got up from the bed and into the bathroom. She stayed in the shower for a long time, her eyes closed against the rush of the water. For a reason she would have found impossible to explain, she needed this time alone. Away from Tiger, away from the beauty of the golden dragon.

When at last she stepped out of the shower she wrapped the clothes she'd worn for almost a week into a bundle, and covering herself with a towel, left the bathroom. She took the half-slip out of the basket and put it on.

"Can we get someone to do the laundry?" she asked Tiger. "Everything is dirty."

"I'll find someone to do it." He put his hands on her shoulders. "You look very tired," he said. "I've sent down to the restaurant for our dinner. After we eat you must rest."

A few minutes later a white-jacketed waiter brought up a tray. He set it on the table and bowed himself out.

Bethany wasn't hungry, but she tried to eat. After only a few spoonfuls of rice and a couple of bites of meat she said, "I'm sorry, Tiger, I just can't eat."

She stood up and when she did he came to her. Putting his hands on her shoulders he kissed her and looked at her strangely. "Is something the matter?" he asked.

"No, of course not." But her voice was uncertain.

Tiger let her go. "I'm going to shower now. Why don't you rest?"

When he closed the bathroom door, Bethany turned back the bedspread and lay down. Pulling the sheet over her, she lay on her side so that she could look at the dragon. Her last thought was of his beauty. Then her eyes closed and she slept.

Chapter 17

Bethany barely awoke when Tiger slipped into the narrow bed beside her. Carefully he put his arm under her head and drew her close. For a moment her body stiffened, then she relaxed and her breathing deepened.

Tiger rested his chin again the softness of her short cropped hair and sighed with the pleasure of having her close again. In a way that he didn't understand, Bethany had been withdrawn since their return from the monastery. He knew of course that she had been as deeply affected by the golden dragon as he had been, as stunned by its beauty. Her gray eyes had widened in astonishment when he unwrapped the statue and her hand had trembled when she reached to touch it. Tiger had looked at her. Then he'd looked at the old monk and he'd been puzzled at the strange smile on the ancient man's face.

Then the moment had passed. The monk had said, "It was in the last days of the war that your fathers came to us. I knew, as everyone in China knew, of the daring exploits of the Flying Tigers. What gallant men they were, those young Americans who risked their lives to protect us. I had the utmost admiration for them, so I was surprised and pleased to meet two of the Tigers in person."

The monk had closed his eyes, remembering. "They were brought to me and when we were alone they said they had a package they would like me to keep for them until after the war. It was the statue of a dragon, they said, and it was very valuable." The old man opened his eyes. "It was in this same box. I did not open it, but I think I knew, even then, what it was. They asked me to keep the statue safe, and because they were the valiant protectors of China, I agreed."

The valiant protectors of China. In the quiet of the night Tiger closed his eyes and tried to conjure up the image of his Irish-American father. Bill Malone had been a tall man with sandy-colored hair, a ruddy complexion and green eyes. He'd talked a lot to his son about his days with the Flying Tigers, of the old P-40's they'd flown, and of the adventures he and his best friend, Ross Adams, had had together.

Tiger had first learned of the dragon's existence when he was ten. They were living in Hong Kong then. He'd come home early from school and as he passed his mother's sitting room he heard his father say, "The dragon belongs to Ross and to me."

His mother, in her cool and haughty voice answered, "No, it does *not*. It belongs to China."

"It belongs to whoever possesses it," his father had roared, his Irish temper flaring. "I'm not going to give up a fortune because you've got some fool notion in that head of yours. One of these days China will open up again and when it does I'm going after the dragon."

A few days later his father had taken him fishing, and he'd told Tiger about the dragon. "I may not make it back to China," Bill said, "what with your mother feeling the way she does. But some day, when you're a man, I want you to go after the statue. It's worth a lot of money, boy, enough to keep you and your mother in style for the rest of your lives."

After his father's death Tiger had discussed with his mother the possibility of taking the statue out of China. But she had been so adamant in her refusal to tell him where it was that he had let the matter drop. Then Bethany had come to Hong Kong; now the golden dragon was theirs.

Tiger looked across the room. By the pale ray of moonlight through the slatted blinds he could see the golden dragon reclining on the other bed. It had come between his father and mother; he would not let it come between Bethany and him. His arms tightened around her. Then he closed his eyes and he too slept.

The cherry trees were in bloom. The delicate flowers made a carpet of white beneath her feet and perfumed the air with their sweet scent. Through the still night she heard the sound of a lute and knew that at last he had come. She pressed her pale hands together, trying to still the frantic beating of her heart as she looked fearfully back at her father's house.

Silently she wept for the days of her childhood and the knowledge that she would never see her mother again. After tonight she would belong to another; she would never return to this house that she had always known. Then she heard his voice and her sadness was forgotten.

Silently, hand in hand, they crept down through the willow trees to the river.

"I have a boat," he told her. "It will take us safely away."

Her hand trembled in his as he brought it to his lips. "Do not be afraid, little bird. With this journey our lives begin."

He led her onto his boat, and with the moon to guide them, they began their journey down the river. They spoke little, but their gazes rested on each other as the boat moved silently through the water. When the hour grew late, he said, "I think I will die if I do not kiss you," and turned the boat toward the shore.

Her heart beat like a captured bird's. The moment had come, the moment that would bind them together for all eternity.

When they reached shallow water he jumped out of the boat and pulled it to the shore. She could smell the jasmine in the air as he took her hand and led her to a place that was hidden by leafy green bamboo. Gently he laid her down there, gently he undressed her. When she lay naked in the moonlight he gazed at the perfection of her body, then dropped to his knees beside her.

"Your skin is as soft as the petal of a rose," he whispered as he touched her cheek. "Your hair drifts like silk through my fingers. Your pomegranate lips await my kiss."

She looked up into his strange green eyes and the night seemed to stand still. From somewhere above them a nightingale sang a song of unutterable sweetness.

"My love," she whispered. "Come to me. Come to me now."

His mouth tasted of honey. She drank in the nectar of it, and sighed with a pleasure she had never known as her pale arms came around his neck to draw him closer.

He touched her breasts and she quivered with desire. Her delicate fingers traced the line of his lips, moved over his shoulders, down to his chest. Her fingers lingered at his waist, trailed delicate patterns over the plane of his hips and stomach and followed the thin trail of hair below his waist.

The breath caught in Tiger's throat. He spoke her name but she stopped his words with her lips. She touched him and he moaned against her mouth. She took his lower lip between her fine white teeth, held it as she ran her tongue back and forth, then took it to suckle before she slipped her tongue into his mouth. And all the while her pale, cool hand caressed him.

Tiger's heart raced as he drew her closer. "Give me your breasts," he whispered, and felt her shiver with the pleasure of his touch. Then her hands were on his shoulders, urging him over her to join his body to hers.

Her body was fire and lightning streaking across the midnight sky. She was wild and wonderful and without restraint as she urged him to peaks of pleasure he had never dreamed possible.

Lost in ecstasy Tiger cried her name. He told her in Chinese how wonderful she was and how he loved the feel of her body against his.

"I know," she whispered. "The feel of your body excites me too."

He touched her silken skin and felt her quickened breath against his throat. "My love," he murmured in Chinese. "Take me to paradise."

"To paradise," she whispered.

Together then, in quickened cadence, they climbed the heights of love, spiraling up and up until their bodies burst with rapture and they clung, heart to heart, in that sweet and final moment of ecstasy.

It was only later, when she slept, that Tiger remembered he had, in the throes of passion, spoken to her in Chinese. And that she had responded.

Bethany awoke slowly the next morning, conscious of the tickle of hair against her cheek and Tiger's slow and steady breathing. She opened her eyes. One hand was curled around Tiger's neck, her face rested against his chest. She frowned, trying to remember when he had joined her in bed. She'd slept so soundly. She remembered looking at the golden dragon, thinking how truly beautiful he was; then she must have drifted off to sleep. The dragon? Her body stiffened. Had she dreamed about him? But no, the dream hadn't been about the dragon, it had been about Flowering Peach and the young poet. About... Suddenly hot color flushed Bethany's cheeks. She raised her head and looked at Tiger. Had they made love? Had she...?

His eyelids fluttered open. A slow smile crossed his face and his arms tightened around her. "Bethany," he whispered. He kissed her and when her mouth trembled under his he told her how wonderful the night had been.

Last night? But last night had been a dream, a dream of Flowering Peach and her lover. It hadn't been real. It wasn't me, she wanted to cry. It was her, that other girl from long ago. But how could she tell him? How could she explain?

Bethany turned her face away so that she could look at the dragon. Its golden body gleamed in the sun. The green eyes looked into hers and she was touched by their sadness. Oh please, her heart cried out. What is it? What do you want?

"Bethany?" Tiger captured her chin and brought her face close to his. He kissed her eyelids closed and feathered soft kisses over her cheeks. "I love you," he whispered against her mouth. "I want to marry you and have children with you."

"Marry...?" Her eyes opened. "Tiger, I don't know. I—"

"You must know how I feel about you, Bethany. I'd like to talk about it now, but if you don't want to then we'll discuss it when we're back in Tsingyun." His arms tightened around her. "But I won't let you go, Bethany. I *am* going to marry you."

Before she could answer Tiger covered her mouth with his, crushing her protests before she could utter them. He *would* have her, he told himself, not just for now, but forever. After last night, after she had given and taken so wildly, so freely, she could not deny that she was his; that he was hers. They were one now, always and forever, united by the bonds of eternal love.

With shaking urgency Tiger said, "I love you, Bethany. I want you, I want you now." He felt her pulling back and suddenly he was bewildered, afraid, unable to understand that the Bethany who'd made such wonderful love to him last night was the Bethany he now held in his arms. He wanted to call her back. He wanted the woman who loved him last night to love him again, soar with him again. "Oh God," Tiger murmured, then with a low cry of need he joined his body to hers. He held her possessively, fiercely, stopping her cry of protest with a kiss as his arms went around her, rocking her to him in an exultation of love. And suddenly Bethany was his again. Her mouth softened, her lips parted. She put her arms around him, held him close and lifted her body to his in complete surrender.

It was too urgent, too fast. It ended in a burst of passion that left them breathless. His body covered hers, he buried his face in the hollow between her throat and shoulder, breathing in the scent of her, knowing that he would never get enough.

They lay for a long time without speaking, still in the position of love, reluctant to part.

"I love you," Tiger said.

"And I love you." Bethany kissed the top of his head. She looked over at the golden dragon. "I love you," she said again.

After their clean clothes were delivered they showered and dressed. "I think it would be all right to go downstairs for breakfast," Tiger said, "but we'd better take the statue with us."

He wrapped it in the scarlet silk and put it back in the box. Then he took Bethany's arm and led her downstairs to the small hotel dining room.

Bethany was silent during breakfast. There was something she had to tell Tiger, but she wasn't sure how to begin.

Over their last cup of tea, Tiger said, "When we finish I'll take you back to the room. Then I'll go to see about our transportation. If there's a flight tonight we'll take it. If not, we'll wait until tomorrow."

Bethany nodded. "It'll be good to get back to Tsingyun," she said. "I've missed your mother."

"I'm glad the two of you like each other." Tiger smiled at her across the table. "I was afraid at first you weren't going to get along."

"So was I." She added sugar to her tea. "We're very different in most ways, Tiger. But in the most important way we're alike."

One dark eyebrow raised. "In what way?"

"We both love you."

Tiger covered her hand with his, but before he could speak, Bethany said, "Tiger, I have to talk to you."

"Of course, Bethany, what is it?"

She shook her head. "Not here."

His gaze met hers across the table. Her gray eyes were serious. He nodded and stood up.

They went back to the room without speaking. When they went in Tiger closed the door. He put the box on the bed and turning to her said, "What is it, Bethany?"

"The dragon." Bethany sank down on the bed and rested her hand on the box. For a moment she didn't speak, then she said, "I don't want to sell him."

Tiger's eyebrows came together in a puzzled frown. "What are you talking about?" He sat down on the bed next to her and took her hand.

"We can't sell him," she said again. "We don't know what would happen to him if we did. What if somebody melted him down for the gold? What if—"

"I doubt anyone would do that, Bethany."

"But we can't be sure."

"No, but—"

"The men who've been after us . . . they're ruthless men, Tiger. They're only interested in the money he'll bring. They're not interested in his beauty, his—"

"His beauty?" Tiger looked at her curiously. "The statue is an *it*, Bethany, not a *him*." He stood up. He walked to the window, then back. "I don't understand you," he said. "We started on this trip with the idea that we were going to get the dragon and return to Hong Kong and sell it. I've wanted to forget it, let it go, but you wouldn't let me. Now you want to give the statue away. You're acting as though the dragon was real, as though it was alive."

Bethany stared at Tiger, then with a cry she covered her face with her hands. She knew she was being ridiculous. The golden dragon was worth a great deal of money and they'd agreed to sell it. But oh God, what if the person they sold it to didn't see his beauty? What if they melted the dragon down for the gold?

"Bethany?" Tiger's hands were on her shoulders. "Tell me," he said, "what is it you want to do with the statue?"

She raised her head and looked at him. "I...I want to give it to a museum," she whispered. "There's one here, we could see it from the monastery. I want to take him there, where everyone can see him and know that love, that the love he and Flowering Peach shared is eternal."

Tiger's hands tightened on her shoulders. He didn't understand what she was saying, but he knew how important this was to her. And how important she was to him. He looked into her tear-filled gray eyes and his heart swelled with love. "All right," he said in a gentle voice. "All right, Bethany, we'll do as you say. We'll give him to the museum."

"Oh, Tiger." Bethany leaned her face against his chest. "Today," she said, "we'll go today."

He nodded. "But first I want to make arrangements for a flight out of here because there may be only one or two a week. I'll see about tickets, then I'll come back and we'll go to the museum." Tiger held her away from him. "If that's really what you want."

"It's what I want," Bethany said.

"But before, when I told you I wanted to give up our pursuit of the dragon you wouldn't agree. What made you change your mind, Bethany?"

"I hadn't seen him then. I didn't know how beautiful he was." With trembling fingers she undid the string around the box, and brushing aside the silk, picked up the golden dragon. He was heavy, but she didn't mind the weight, for again it seemed to her that she could feel the quiver of life beneath her fingertips. "He doesn't belong to us, Tiger," she said softly. "He belongs to China."

Tiger touched her cropped black hair. He knew that he loved Bethany more in that moment than he'd ever thought it possible to love anyone. He watched as she put the dragon on the bed. He saw the way her fingers lingered on the statue's face as she tenderly traced the tear that marred the golden cheek.

"I want you to stay here and lock the door behind me," he said when he got to his feet. "I don't know how long I'll be. I'm going to the airline office and that usually takes a lot of time here in China."

Bethany smiled up at him. Now that she had made the decision she felt as though a great weight had been lifted from her shoulders. When Tiger took her hands and pulled her up, she went willingly into his arms.

"I'm asking you to give up a great deal, Tiger," Bethany said. "I know how valuable the statue is, I know the kind of financial security it could give you. But I feel . . . I know that this is the right thing to do."

Tiger kissed her. "So do I, Bethany."

"Thank you, Tiger."

He held her for a moment, then, reluctantly, let her go. "I may be gone for several hours," he said. "Stay here, Bethany. I don't want you out on the street without me."

"I won't leave."

"And lock the door."

"I will." She kissed his cheek. He opened the door and stood for a moment looking at her. "Lock the door behind me," he said again.

Bethany listened to his steps receding down the corridor. It's going to be all right, she thought. We'll take the golden dragon to the museum where he'll be safe, where other lovers will see him.

With a happy sigh Bethany went to stand by the window. She looked out at the busy street, waiting for Tiger to emerge from the hotel. When she saw him she smiled and thought how much she loved him and of the life they would have together.

Then Bethany's smile faded. She gasped and her hands tightened on the window sill. Two men stood by a lamppost. They were watching Tiger. She'd seen them before. One of them had been driving the car when she'd been kidnapped; the other man she'd seen on the train just before she jumped.

Bethany cried a warning, even though she knew Tiger couldn't hear her. But the men didn't go after Tiger; they only watched, and waited until he disappeared into the crowd.

The man from the train said something to the other man. Then they walked across the street toward the hotel. One entered, the other positioned himself at the corner of the busy street. They were coming here! After the dragon. After her.

Bethany stood frozen, then with an anguished cry she picked up the golden dragon and put him into the wicker basket. They mustn't get him. They mustn't! She jammed the Mao hat on her head, took the basket, and without a backward look fled from the room.

Chapter 18

Bethany ran down the hall to the back stairs. There was no door, only the open stairs leading down to the working part of the hotel. As she plunged down them she heard footsteps running in the corridor above.

She ran, clutching the heavy basket in one hand, the railing with the other. Almost at the bottom she heard a shout from above, and looking up saw the man from the train peering down from the top of the stairwell. With a cry of terror Bethany leaped down the rest of the stairs and when she reached the door at the bottom flung it open. She was in an empty laundry room. Jumping over piles of dirty laundry, she ran through the room, saw another door and pushed it open.

Startled faces looked up from soup pots and steaming kettles. Bethany glanced quickly around the kitchen, frantic to find a way out, knowing the man from the train would follow her in here. She ran around a table where a cook in a tall hat was slicing vegetables. He shouted something and waved his knife at her, but she ignored him as she looked around searching for a way out. Suddenly, the door she'd entered burst open. Voices raised to an excited pitch as a man with a gun burst into the kitchen.

Bethany ran around the table. She saw a door and headed for it, pushing the vegetable man out of the way as she glanced over her shoulder. The man from the train was only a few steps behind her. She darted around a stove that held a pot of steaming soup, gave it a shove with her free hand, then spurted ahead as the steaming liquid caught her pursuer. He screamed as she raced through the door, up a short flight of stairs, to the street.

Gasping for breath, aware that her hand was burned but not caring, Bethany looked up and down the street. Suddenly she froze. The other man, the chauffeur of the car that had kidnapped her, stood only a yard or two away, looking up at the hotel. Her hand tightened around the handle of the basket. The man from the kitchen, unless he was badly hurt, would come through the door behind any second now. She had to get away.

Be calm, she told herself. Be calm. She pulled the cap lower on her face, then taking a deep breath, stepped out onto the crowded street.

Bethany made herself walk without seeming haste past other pedestrians. Keep your head down, she told herself. Don't panic. Don't— A shout went up behind her. She darted a glance over her shoulder. The man who'd been after her in the hotel, a towel clutched to his face, was with the chauffeur who'd been positioned at the corner. He screamed in anger and pointed toward her.

Bethany plunged past the people in front of her, pushing them aside as she raced toward the end of the street. At the corner she paused, stopped, saw a narrow alley and ran into it. Other, smaller passageways, branched off the alley. She ran on, scarcely aware of the heavy burden she carried. I'll be all right if I can get to the end of the alley before they see me, she told herself. She was almost there, another few steps and she'd... She stopped. My God, there wasn't any exit! She was caught in a dead-end passage. Behind her she heard a shout.

Bethany looked wildly around, then, without conscious thought, turned into one of the passageways, opened the nearest door and plunged inside.

An old man was bent over a sewing machine. He looked up, startled, then said something she didn't understand.

"Two men are after me," Bethany cried. "Please help me. Please..." And almost wept in frustration because she knew the tailor didn't understand her.

He got up from his machine and began waving his arms at her.

"Please," Bethany said again. "Please help me."

Heavy footsteps were running in the passageway, angry voices were raised as fists began pounding on the neighboring doors. In another moment they'd be at the tailor's door. They'd have her; they'd have the golden dragon.

Feeling as though her heart would surely burst from her chest, Bethany searched frantically for an escape. The old man grabbed her arm. He spoke again, but she didn't understand. Skinny fingers dug into her arm. He pulled her after him and she had no choice but to follow him as he led her to a corner of the room and pulled back a rug. He lifted a small brass ring, opened a two-foot-wide trapdoor and beckoned to her.

For a moment Bethany hesitated. Someone pounded on the door. She glanced at the tailor and quickly lowered herself into the opening. The door closed over her head. She heard him shuffle away and cry out in an impatient voice. Then other voices, angry voices.

Bethany huddled in the dark, narrow space, sure the men above could hear the frantic beating of her heart. She'd never known such darkness, such fear. For a moment she wanted to cry out so that she could escape from this frightening place. But if she did they'd take the dragon. She closed her eyes and tried to force herself to calmness.

With shaking hands Bethany clutched the dragon. She took a deep breath. The frantic beating of her heart slowed. She moved the satin wrapping aside so that she could touch him. He was cool against her fingertips, and she held him against her breast.

There were angry shouts above. Noises of furniture being overturned. A cry. Bethany flinched, but she didn't move. She just held the dragon close and waited.

After what seemed an eternity the shouting stopped. The steps receded. There was only silence, and darkness. Bethany waited. She had to be sure her pursuers had gone. Ten minutes went by. She wrapped the dragon in the silk and put him back in the basket. Her legs were cramped, sweat ran down her body. She felt above her head and with the flat of her hand tried to lift the trapdoor. It didn't budge. Frightened, she put both hands against the door and pushed as hard as she could. It lifted. She raised it an inch and peered out, stifling a cry as she surveyed the room. It was a shambles. Tables were overturned, the material the tailor had been working on was strewn across the floor. He lay beside his machine.

With every bit of her strength, grunting with the effort, Bethany pushed the trapdoor all the way open. She climbed out, then reached down for the basket with the dragon. Quickly she ran and knelt beside the old man. He was unconscious, and a trickle of blood ran down the side of his face. She felt for the pulse in his neck. It was weak but steady. She got up to look around for water. Seeing a spigot and a pail, she ran some water, found a cloth, and hurrying to the tailor's side, bathed his face.

"Please," Bethany said. "Oh, please, be all right." She patted his face. "Sir? Sir, can you hear me? Wake up. They've gone now. Oh, please . . ."

His eyelids fluttered open. He groaned and tried to sit up.

"No," Bethany said. "Rest a moment. Don't try to move yet." She bathed the wound on his head, then quickly ran to get him a drink of water and held his head while he drank. This was her fault. The tailor had tried to protect her. He'd been hurt because he wouldn't tell the men where she was. She folded some material and put it under his head for a pillow. He murmured something she didn't understand and tried to smile. He closed his eyes and in a little while he slept.

Bethany sat beside him, a worried frown on her face. She took his pulse again; it seemed stronger.

For a long time Bethany sat beside the tailor. Every few minutes she checked his pulse. Finally she got up and began to straighten the shop, righting the overturned tables and the chair, picking up the scattered material, folding it neatly. The table with the sewing machine on it was the only one that hadn't been overturned. When the shop had been put to rights, she went back and sat on the floor beside the tailor.

Bethany didn't know how much time had elapsed since she'd fled the hotel. If Tiger had returned he must be frantic with worry. As soon as she made sure the old man was all right she'd go back to the hotel. She... But no, she couldn't go back. The men who were looking for her would be waiting there. She had to go somewhere else. But where? Dear God, where could she go where both she and the dragon would be safe?

If only she understood Chinese. If only she could call Tiger and warn him. If only... At last, exhausted by all that had happened, Bethany closed her eyes and slept.

When she awoke she saw the tailor standing next to a one-burner hot plate. "Are you all right?" she asked as she got quickly to her feet.

He spoke quickly, bowed several times, then handed her a cup of tea. Smiling her thanks, Bethany took the cup. It was black tea, strong and good, and with each sip she felt the strength flow back into her body. She knew now where she and the dragon would be safe. The monastery, she'd go to the monastery, and some way, from there, she'd get word to Tiger.

After the tea was finished Bethany thanked the old tailor, even though she knew he didn't understand.

He bowed and spoke. His meaning was lost to Bethany, but she took his hand and by her expression tried to show him how grateful she was for his kindness.

He went to the door and peered out. With a nod he motioned her forward.

"Thank you," she said again, as she picked up the basket and stepped out into the passageway.

A late afternoon gloom had settled over the city as cautiously, head lowered, Bethany went down the alley. When she reached the street she merged with the people who were walking there. The monastery, she thought, I've got to get to the monastery. She raised her eyes and looked at the distant hills.

She had no money so she'd have to go on foot. The golden dragon was heavy. She walked for blocks until she reached the edge of town, then began to climb. An hour later, too exhausted to go on, she stopped beneath a tree and sinking to the ground, rested. Soon it would be dark. She closed her eyes for a moment, then with a sigh got to her feet.

The road wound up the high hill. It was quiet here away from the noise of the city. Bethany wiped the perspiration from her face and shifted the basket to her other hand. With the last rays of sun she could see the Yangtze River. She leaned her back against a tree and flexed her arms that ached from the weight of the dragon. She didn't know how much farther she had to go.

When night closed in around Bethany, she stayed at the edge of the road. One step at a time, she told herself. The stars came out, a quarter moon appeared. She rested again, and without meaning to closed her eyes. Then jerking awake, she made herself get up and go on.

"We'll make it," she said to the dragon as she staggered to her feet. "You'll be safe tonight and tomorrow we'll take you to the museum, and all of us who have ever loved will see you there and know that your love, that all true love is eternal."

She fell to her knees and when she raised her head she saw through the darkness the flickering lights of the monastery. With a glad cry she stood up and with both hands lifted the heavy basket.

Her gaze on the lights ahead, Bethany marched on. An hour passed. Her legs and arms trembled with fatigue. The lights grew closer, the air grew chill. She went on without thinking, one foot ahead of the other, one weary step at a time. Suddenly the tall iron gate loomed in front of her, and for a reason she could not explain, she began to weep. She reached for the bell rope and at the sound of the bell sank slowly to the ground.

A monk bent over her. He held a cup of steaming soup to her lips.

"Where am I? What...?" Bethany tried to sit up but he restrained her.

"Drink," the monk said in English.

Bethany did as she was told. The broth tasted of chicken and noodles. When she'd finished half of it she said, "Thank you. I feel better now."

She was in a clean, small room, resting on a straw mat. The wicker basket had been placed on the floor beside her.

"We found you at the gate," another monk said from the only chair in the room. "You were unable to walk and we brought you here. You must finish your soup and then you will sleep."

"I have to get word to someone."

"In the morning."

"But he'll be frantic with worry. Please. His name is Malone, Tiger Malone. He's at the Hotel of the Swallows in room 402. You must get word to him."

The monk beside her turned to look at the other man. "I will ask Saka Muni Buddha," he said as he rose to his feet. To Bethany he said, "Sleep now, my child. I will leave the candle so that you are not alone in the dark."

Before Bethany could protest, the two monks went out and closed the door.

She was alone in this silent room. "Tiger," she whispered. What had he thought when he returned to the hotel to find her gone? Was he safe? My God, what if the two men who had been after her had attacked him? She covered her face with her arm. Oh please, she prayed, let him be safe. Let Tiger be safe.

As the first light of dawn crept in through the window above her head, Bethany opened her eyes. Before she could sit up there was a knock. When she said, "Come in," the same monk who had given her the broth the night before entered with a cup of tea.

"Drink this," he said, "then I will take you to Saka Muni Buddha."

Bethany ran her fingers through her tousled hair. "Has Mr. Malone been told that I'm here?"

"I believe he has." The monk folded his arms inside the wide sleeves of his robe and did not speak again until Bethany had finished her tea. "Please come," he said then.

She picked up the wicker basket and followed him out to the long, silent hall and the open corridor that bordered a flower-filled patio. The early morning air was cool, and a mist hung over the garden. It was so quiet here, so peaceful and beautiful. In spite of her concern for Tiger, Bethany felt that peace penetrate her very being.

The monk stopped before the tall, carved door, knocked and when a voice spoke he opened the door.

The old monk once again looked at Bethany from behind his desk. "You have come back. I knew that you would." He motioned her to a chair and said, "I have sent word to Mr. Malone. He will be here soon."

"He's all right then." Bethany half rose from her chair. "Thank God."

"You have brought the statue?"

"Yes, I have." Her arms tightened around the basket.

"You are protective of it." The old eyes narrowed as he measured her. "You are afraid someone will steal it and you know it is worth a great deal of money."

"I'm afraid someone will steal it," Bethany said, "but not because of money."

"Then why?" His eyes burned into hers.

"Because his value is priceless."

"Ah."

"His value to China. Because of what he represents."

In a voice that crackled with age the monk said, "You refer to a statue, an *object*, as he. I find that strange." His lips formed a mocking smile. "And what does *he* represent?"

"Love."

The monk looked at her from across his desk. "Just so," he whispered. "Just so."

"We have decided to give the dragon to the museum here. He doesn't belong to us, he belongs to China."

It was silent in the room, but the silence was strangely comforting. From a distance Bethany heard the bell at the gate. She took a deep breath and knew that it was Tiger and that he was safe. When at last she heard footsteps in the corridor she stood and faced the door. A monk opened it and she saw Tiger.

"Bethany!" He reached her in three strides. "You're all right! They didn't hurt you?"

"No, Tiger, I'm all right."

"When I got back to the hotel and found you gone..." He put his arms on her shoulders and looked at her. "I thought they had you," he murmured. "I was crazy with worry until early this morning when a messenger arrived."

Tiger let her go and turning to the old monk said, "I'm sorry, sir. Forgive my rudeness. Thank you for giving refuge to Miss Adams."

"This is a place of refuge." The old man smiled. "I expected you sooner."

Holding Bethany's hand, Tiger approached the desk and said, "The men who were after Miss Adams were at the hotel when I returned yesterday afternoon. They were waiting for me in the room." He looked at Bethany. "I started to open the door. I had my hand on the knob, and I sensed something...something I can't explain. I spoke your name, Bethany, so low that even I could barely hear it. And I knew, I knew something wasn't right. I pulled back, then I ran in, low. The man from the train was behind the door. He had a gun. I grabbed it and wrestled him to the floor before his partner jumped me."

Tiger put his hand against Bethany's cheek. "I went crazy," he said. "All I could think about was what they had done with you. I wanted to kill them."

"But you did not," the monk said.

"No, I didn't. I managed to overpower them and send for the police. They're in custody now."

"Thank God." Bethany sank down onto a chair. "Who were they, Tiger? How did they know about the dragon?"

"It all goes back a long time, Bethany, back to the warlord who gave it to our fathers, to the men who tortured and killed him. The police told me there was a whole group of them in those days, a kind of Chinese Mafia that specialized in stealing works of art and ancient artifacts." He looked at the monk. "But it's over now, they're behind bars. And so is their leader, Weng Tsan Tsi."

"Weng Tsan Tsi!" The monk rose from his chair. "He is a scourge, a vulture. He has fed off the heritage of China for decades."

"Not any more," Tiger said. "He was apprehended in Beijing this morning."

"Is it over?" Bethany asked. "Is it really over? Will the dragon be safe now?"

"It will be safe," Tiger said. "And so will we." He looked down at her, then with a frown asked, "But I don't understand, Bethany. How did you know they were after us? How did you escape from the hotel?"

"I saw them from the window when you left. Tiger, I was so afraid because I thought they meant to follow you. But they didn't. One of them, the man from the train, came into the hotel, the other man waited outside. I didn't know what to do so I grabbed the dragon and ran down the back stairs."

Bethany paused to get her breath. "They almost caught me. I ran into a shop and a tailor helped me—he hid me." She looked up at Tiger. "I want to see him again. I want to thank him for what he did for me."

"But how did you get here, Bethany?"

"I walked."

"You walked?" Tiger stared at her, disbelieving. "You carried the golden dragon all the way up here?"

Bethany nodded. "I knew he'd be safe here."

"But the statue is almost too heavy for me. How did you manage?"

"She managed with love," the old monk said as he smiled at Bethany.

And Bethany smiled back, because in some strange way he knew, this ancient Saka Muni Buddha with the skin like old parchment knew how she felt about the golden dragon.

Then she looked at Tiger. She went to him and put her hands on his shoulders. "Now we must give the dragon back," she said, "back to the people of China."

Chapter 19

The morning was bright and clear when Bethany and Tiger climbed the hill of Eternal Spring. The road was bordered by tall white birch and pink mimosa trees. Scarlet peonies circled a pond where water lilies sparkled in the sunlight.

"This is where he should be," Bethany said.

Tiger looked at her. He didn't understand this feeling Bethany had for the dragon, but he knew that Bethany had fallen under its spell from the moment she'd seen it. Her gray eyes had widened with shock, her fingers had trembled when she touched it.

He too had been stunned by the statue's beauty and its value. But Bethany hadn't seen the value, she'd seen only the beauty and its connection with the legend his mother had told them that evening in the garden at Tsingyun—the legend of the young girl named

Flowering Peach and of the poet who had played to
her on his lute and told her of his love.

Tiger looked down at Bethany as she moved a little
away from him to stand in the shade of one of the mimosa trees. She'd taken the cap off, and the sun shone
on her face. Suddenly, chokingly, Tiger's heart was so
filled with love that it almost overwhelmed him. He
put down the heavy box and went to her. Before she
could speak he put his arms around her and drew her
close.

"I love you, Bethany," he said. "I will always love
you."

She touched his face. "As I will always love you,"
she whispered. She closed her eyes and rested her face
against his chest.

They stood like that for a moment in the shade of
the tree. Tiger looked at her for another moment, then
he picked up the box and together they walked the final steps to the museum.

The curator received them in his office. A middle-
aged man with a sensitive, ascetic face, he looked to
Bethany like a Mandarin scholar. He stood and
bowed, and in careful English said to her, "You are
not Chinese?"

"No, I'm American."

He nodded, then looking from one to the other of
them asked, "How may I help you?"

"We have brought something that we would like to
give to your museum—if you would like to have it."
Tiger placed the box on the curator's desk.

"I see." The curator motioned for them to be
seated. "That is most kind of you, sir and lady. We
have in this museum only the finest artifacts of our

ancient Chinese civilization." He hesitated. "From time to time people wish to donate. I do not like to seem ungrateful, but we do not accept everything that is offered."

"I understand," Tiger said. "May I show you what we have brought?"

"Of course." The curator leaned back in his chair, his long, slender fingers pointed together in a pyramid shape, his jet-black eyes on the box.

Tiger opened the box, folded back the silk, and taking the golden dragon in both his hands, placed it on the desk.

The curator's gasp was audible in the silent room. He did not speak as he got slowly to his feet. He murmured something in Chinese and ran his hands over the statue. "It is the dragon." His voice was awed. "The golden dragon." He looked from Tiger to Bethany. "Where . . . ? How did you get it?"

"It came into our fathers' possession during the war with the Japanese," Tiger said. "It has been hidden away for forty years."

The curator nodded. "I knew that it had disappeared." His gaze returned to the dragon. "I have heard about this statue all of my life but I never expected to have the good fortune to see it. When I was a boy in Guilin my mother told me a legend about the dragon. I have never forgotten it."

"The story of Flowering Peach and the young poet," Bethany said.

"You too know the story?"

"I believe the story," she said.

The curator's dark eyes softened. "I did, too, when I was a child. But when I grew older I realized it was just a story. Now . . . now I look at its beauty, its magnificence, and I must pause to wonder.''

"You will take it?" Tiger asked.

The curator nodded. "Yes, most kind sir, I will take him."

Him. Bethany took a deep breath and a feeling of peace settled upon her heart. She looked at the curator. "Thank you," she said.

"It is I who thank you, dear lady." He came around his desk, and bowing, took Bethany's hand. "He will be safe here, his legend will live on."

Tiger looked from the curator to Bethany. He didn't understand the almost mystical attraction that the dragon seemed to have for Bethany and the curator. He only knew that he loved Bethany and that parting with the dragon made her sad. But the face that turned to him wasn't sad, it was filled with happiness.

I will never understand her, Tiger thought, but I will always love her.

That evening, as the shadows lengthened over the Yangtze, Tiger and Bethany flew from Chungtai to Shanghai. They took a taxi to the International Hotel and were shown to a room that was the most luxurious they'd had since they left Tsingyun. It was furnished with a double bed, a dresser, a table and a chair, and had windows that looked out on the People's Park. When Bethany went to stand by the window, Tiger put his hands on her shoulders.

Resting his chin against her hair he said, "We'll stay here for a few days, and I'll show you the city of Shanghai."

"Can we go shopping tomorrow? I want to get out of these clothes before I actually turn into a boy."

"I think there is little danger of that ever happening." Tiger put a finger under her chin and raised her face for his kiss. "Very little danger."

He felt Bethany's lips curve in a smile and tightened his arms around her. We're safe now, he thought as he kissed her. No more running, no more looking over our shoulders. Her lips were soft, her body warm against his.

"I love you," Tiger said, then he picked her up in his arms and carried her to the bed.

When he had undressed her, and himself, they lay close, without speaking, content for the moment to let passion wait. Tiger brushed the hair back from her face and she said, "I'd like to find a beauty shop, one that can change my hair back to its natural color."

He kissed the top of her head. "We'll find one tomorrow." Then he chuckled. "It would be a shock to Mother if she could see the way you looked now."

"She's probably sick with worry. We must phone her."

"We will tomorrow." Tiger turned her face up to his. "But tonight is ours, Bethany." He kissed her, and in his kiss there was love and longing and the promise of all the nights that were to come.

Bethany's lips parted under his. Her arms crept around his neck to draw him closer as the sweet, familiar fire crept through her body. Her tongue darted to meet his, her hands tightened on his shoulders. She felt the whole wonderfully masculine length of his body against hers and her heart surged, knowing the pleasure that awaited her in his arms.

Tiger rained kisses on her face and murmured her name. His hands were strong as they moved slowly down her body. He kissed her breasts and she whispered her pleasure, carried higher and higher on the wings of his love.

"My dear love," he said as he joined his body to hers. Together then, clinging and close, they moved to a rhythm older than time, then soaring to the heights, they tumbled breathless back to the warmth of each other's arms.

The next morning Tiger called Su Ching. "Bethany and I are in Shanghai," he said. "It's over, Mother, we're safe now."

"Thank God." He heard the relief in his mother's voice. "When are you and Bethany coming home?"

"In a few days. We're going to rest here in Shanghai."

"You found the dragon? You have it now?"

"We found it, Mother, but we don't have it."

"I don't understand."

"We gave it to a museum in Chungtai."

The line was silent. When Su Ching spoke she was weeping. In a low voice she managed to say, "At last." Then she said, "I love you, Tiger. I am proud that you are my son."

She asked to speak to Bethany, and when Bethany took the phone Su Ching said, "Was it what you wanted, too?"

"Yes, Su Ching. The golden dragon is where he should be. The legend will live on."

For a long moment Su Ching did not answer, but when at last she spoke there was great happiness in her voice. "Come home, Bethany," she said. "Come home, my dear."

That day Tiger and Bethany shopped along Nanjing Road. They bought two Western-style dresses for her, as well as shoes and a bag; for Tiger, a shirt, jacket and trousers. Later they had lunch, then walked along the Bund and through small parks along the edge of the Yellow River.

It was peaceful there and they lingered as twilight settled over the ancient city. When it grew dark they went back to their hotel, to their room with the double bed. They made love, and slept, and woke to make love again.

The next day Bethany dressed in a pale-green summer cotton and high-heeled sandals. It felt strange, she thought as she looked in the mirror, to be dressed this way. She looked at the Mao cap she'd worn for so long, and with a smile put it in the new suitcase. She'd give the other clothes away, but she'd never part with the cap.

After breakfast they found a beauty shop. The technician, a small, birdlike woman, looked in horror at Bethany's hair. She fluttered around Bethany, touched her hair, shook her head, then picked up scissors and comb and went to work, muttering in Chinese all the while. At last, satisfied with her handiwork, she led Bethany to a booth and covered her head with an evil-smelling solution. Thirty minutes later she washed the solution off and turned Bethany toward a mirror.

The blond was lighter than her natural shade, but it looked a thousand times better than the black dye she'd lived with for the past weeks.

When Bethany dressed and came out into the waiting room of the salon, Tiger glanced up from the magazine he'd been reading, then continued reading.

"Tiger?"

He lowered the magazine again. "My God," he said. "Is it you?"

Bethany smiled. "How do you like it?"

"You're . . . you look wonderful." He lowered his voice. "It's almost as though the other you never existed."

"The other me existed," Bethany said. "I'll never forget the way it was."

They arrived in Tsingyun at the end of the week. It was September now and the leaves were beginning to turn. They took a pedicab to his mother's home. She greeted them at the door and led them into the living room.

"Let us have some tea," Su Ching said, "then you will tell me everything that has happened." She touched Bethany's hand. "You've cut your hair. You're thinner. Are you all right?"

"Yes, Su Ching, I'm fine." Bethany took the proffered cup of tea and smiled at the older woman. Looking around the room she said, "It's good to be back."

"I have been frantic with worry. Why didn't you telephone or send a message, Tiger?"

"We were followed, Mother, almost from the time we left here. I thought it would be safer for you if we did not try to communicate. I'm sorry, I know you were worried." He looked at Bethany and with his gaze on her said to his mother, "When Bethany said she wanted to give the dragon to the Chungtai museum, I knew you would be pleased."

Su Ching put her teacup on the lacquer table. "It is a beautiful thing you have done, Bethany, and I must confess that I did not expect you to do it. You are not Chinese and you cannot understand our close ties with our ancient culture. We are a superstitious people; some of us believe in our legends."

"I know." Bethany smiled at Su Ching over her cup of tea. "So do some of us infidels."

Su Ching chuckled. "You are a remarkable woman, Bethany Adams," she said. "For an infidel."

Tiger looked from his mother to Bethany, not quite sure he understood this communication that flowed between them. But he was grateful that it was there, and that the two people he loved most in the world had such a strong bond.

That night, under the apricot tree in his mother's courtyard, Tiger asked Bethany to marry him.

She looked at him, and for a heart-stopping moment he couldn't breathe. "I love you," he said. "I want to spend the rest of my life with you. I want to have children with you."

Bethany leaned her face against his chest. In this strange and foreign land with a man who was different from any man she'd ever known, she felt very far away from the home she had always known. If she married him her life would never be the same. She would no longer be Bethany Adams from Tiffin, Ohio. She would be Tiger's wife, a part of his world. Such a different world.

From somewhere out of her past came the words: to lose the earth you know for greater knowing, to lose the life you have for greater living, to leave the friends you loved for greater loving.

For greater loving. Bethany raised her face and looked into Tiger's green eyes. "Yes," she said. "Yes, my darling, of course I'll marry you."

When Bethany opened her eyes she thought, today is my wedding day. Today I become Mrs. Tiger Malone.

She had seen little of Tiger since the night they told his mother they were going to be married. Su Ching had embraced them and then she had banished Tiger from the house.

"It is not proper for you to be here," she said. "You will stay with Great-Uncle Chan until the day of the ceremony."

"But Mother," Tiger protested, "Bethany and I only want a small ceremony. We will be married in the registry and—"

"You will have a proper Chinese wedding," Su Ching said firmly. "All of our relatives will attend so that they may wish you and Bethany well, and weep, and drink great quantities of rice wine at the banquet you will give."

Tiger groaned. "Mother, please. We—"

"A Chinese wedding," Su Ching said. "Now pack your things. I will inform Great-Uncle that you are coming to stay with him."

During the following two weeks Bethany saw Tiger only twice. Both times his mother had been present. She had met dozens of uncles and aunts. This morning three of the female cousins were coming to help her dress.

Su Ching had helped Bethany select the material for her wedding dress. When Bethany pointed to a lovely white brocade Su Ching looked horrified. "Impossible," she said. "Red is the marriage color."

It was Bethany's turn to look horrified. "Red?" she'd exploded. "I absolutely will not be married in red."

They had compromised on pink for the ceremony and red silk for the banquet to follow. The wedding dress, made in the style of a Chinese robe, fell to Bethany's ankles and had a high neck, and wide flowing sleeves. It wasn't her idea of what a wedding dress should be but she knew it was useless to argue with Tiger's mother. Until she was married, Su Ching would tell her what to do and she would do it. She was grateful that Su Ching had permitted Tiger to come for dinner the previous evening.

He'd been very formal. He'd kissed his mother's cheek, then Bethany's hand, and said, "I look forward to tomorrow with great joy."

"Just so," Su Ching had replied.

When they were seated at the dinner table, Tiger had poured rice wine into small porcelain cups. Raising his he'd said, "To the two most beautiful women in China." Then, to Su Ching: "I have something I would like to give Bethany, Mother."

She nodded. "You have my permission."

"Thank you." Tiger tried not to smile as he took an ivory box out of his pocket and placed it in Bethany's hand.

Bethany looked at him, then she opened the box. The jade ring and the matching earrings were set in gold. Bedazzled, she stared at them. She handed the ring to Tiger and in a tremulous voice said, "Will you put it on my finger?"

He took her hand in his and for a moment it seemed as though the two of them were alone. He kissed her palm, then turning her hand slipped the jade ring on the third finger of her left hand.

"I love you, Bethany," he said.

When the meal was over Su Ching had risen and said, "Good night, Tiger. We will see you tomorrow."

He had looked longingly at Bethany; then, with a sigh, said, "Yes, Mother, tomorrow."

Now it was tomorrow.

The three young cousins arrived before Bethany finished her tea. They were as bright and cheerful as a flock of magpies. It didn't matter that Bethany didn't understand a word they said, they chattered on, stifling giggles behind lovely white hands. They helped her bathe, washed her hair and rinsed it in perfumed lotus water. When her hair was dry, and after she had applied her makeup, the cousins brushed the short blond hair back from her face and pinned pearls and columbine among the soft curls.

After they helped her into the dress and slipped pink satin shoes on her feet, they led her to the full-length mirror and stood back, waiting for her reaction.

Bethany looked at herself for a moment, then she went to each of the cousins and kissed their smooth cheeks.

It was time.

Tiger arrived. He wore a red robe and cloak and Bethany thought he looked very foreign and very handsome.

"You are more beautiful that I ever imagined," he said as he took off his scarlet cloak and placed it over Bethany's shoulders. "I will keep the image of the way you look today forever in my heart."

Then he bowed to Su Ching. "Great-uncle Chan is waiting in the taxi. Shall we go?"

The four of them went to the registrar's office for the brief, formal ceremony and the signing of the official papers. From the registry they proceeded by pedicab to a temple where the traditional Chinese ceremony would take place. Just before they stepped from the cab Su Ching fastened a sheer red silk handkerchief over Bethany's face. "This is the tradition," she said.

Tiger held her hand during the ceremony. He looked into her eyes and spoke to her in Chinese. It didn't matter that Bethany didn't understand the words. She saw the love in Tiger's face and listened with her heart.

When the ceremony was over Tiger took the veil from Bethany's face. He looked at her with tenderness and love and gently kissed her lips.

When they returned to his mother's home, Mai Ling brought tea and Tiger said, "We must kneel and serve my mother tea, Bethany. Then she will serve us wine that has been sweetened with honey."

Bethany knelt beside him. Mai Ling placed a tray before them. Together they filled the cup, gave it to Su Ching, and saw the joy in her heart light up her face. She sipped the tea, then rose, and going to a sideboard filled a golden goblet with wine, and poured honey into another goblet. Then Great-uncle Chan lighted incense and placed two tall red candles on a table. When the candles were lighted Tiger and Bethany knelt again.

Su Ching took a red ribbon, connected the two goblets and held them out to Bethany and Tiger. "May you always find sweetness in your love," she said.

Tiger sipped from one cup, Bethany from the other. Then they exchanged cups and drank again.

When they arose the three cousins came in to take Bethany upstairs. They dressed her in the red gown of happiness, took the columbine and pearls from her hair, and pinned in red carnations.

They rode to the banquet in red sedan chairs to the accompaniment of musicians. At the banquet they feasted and drank rice wine, and for dessert ate moon cakes and sweet lotus seeds. As soon as they'd finished, although the revelry continued, Tiger took Bethany's hand. With a formal bow he thanked his mother and his relatives. Then, amid giggles and jokes that Bethany didn't understand, he led her out to a waiting sedan chair.

The night was quiet as he slipped his arm around her waist and drew her close. When they reached his mother's house they went together out into the courtyard. Through the blossoms of the apricot trees Bethany could see the beginning of a new moon. She moved closer to Tiger. "My wife," he said. "My dear wife."

He kissed her then. And it seemed to Bethany that in the distance she heard the faint and haunting sound of a lute.

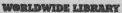

Silhouette Intimate Moments

COMING NEXT MONTH

#197 FOOL'S MUSIC—Mary Lynn Baxter

Lauren DeCoty was on a modeling assignment in France when she was abducted. To Lauren's horror, one of her kidnappers was Ry Kincaid—her first and only love. Ry promised to protect her, but who would keep her from losing her heart—again?

#198 COMMAND PERFORMANCE—Nora Roberts

Eve always thought of Alexander de Cordina as a fairy-tale prince from a magical kingdom. Then she discovered that Alexander was a man of flesh and blood and passionate feelings—and that the land of happily ever after held a danger that was frighteningly real.

#199 THE DREAMING—Amanda Stevens

Except in her dreams, Toni Sinclair had no time for romance—until she went on vacation in Egypt. There she met David Spaulding, then found herself fleeing from an attacker, not sure if she could trust the man she loved.

#200 MISTRESS OF CLIFF HOUSE—Jeanne Stephens

In the past, Cassie Underwood had loved visiting Cliff House, but this time her nights were haunted by footsteps, and her days were disturbed by Daniel Reardon. Cassie suspected Daniel of theft: her grandmother's papers and jewels were missing—and so was Cassie's heart.

AVAILABLE THIS MONTH:

ATTRACTIVE, SPACE SAVING BOOK RACK

Display your most prized novels on this handsome and sturdy book rack. The hand-rubbed walnut finish will blend into your library decor with quiet elegance, providing a practical organizer for your favorite hard-or soft-covered books.

Only $9.95

Approximately 16" x 8" when assembled

Assembles in seconds!

To order, rush your name, address and zip code, along with a check or money order for $10.70* ($9.95 plus 75¢ postage and handling) payable to *Silhouette Books.*

> Silhouette Books
> Book Rack Offer
> 901 Fuhrmann Blvd.
> P.O. Box 1325
> Buffalo, NY 14269-1325

> *Offer not available in Canada.*

*New York residents add appropriate sales tax.

BKR-2R